ALSO BY SCOTT WARREN

The Sorcerous Crimes Division:
Devilbone

VICK'S VULTURES

SCOTT WARREN

PARVUS
fantasy + science fiction

Parvus Press, LLC

PO Box 711232
Herndon, VA 20171
ParvusPress.com

Vick's Vultures
Copyright © 2016 by Scott Warren

Parvus Press supports our authors and encourages creatives of all stripes. If you have questions about fair use, duplication, or how to obtain library copies, please visit our website. Thank you for purchasing this title and supporting the numerous people who worked to bring it together for your enjoyment.

3:1 harbors are a suckers bet, go for 2:1 brick instead.

ISBN 13 978-0-9976613-1-6
Ebook ISBN 978-0-9976613-0-9

Cover art by Tom Edwards Design
Designed and typeset by Catspaw DTP Services
Author photo credit by Rebecca Shelton and Taylor Loy

PROLOGUE

ATOMIC FIRE BLOSSOMED, whiting out the rear-facing sensors of the *Dreadstar*. First Prince Tavram scowled as his final Malagath warship disappeared from the battle reader, spent to allow him the opportunity to escape. A regrettable sacrifice, if necessary. Avoidable? Perhaps. Foreseeable? Absolutely not; this convoy was a secret even from the admiralty. Conclusion? Betrayal. The ambush had been swift and perfect. Likewise, the retribution would be equally so, in due time. For now, survival in the next few moments became the paramount task.

The Dirregaunt mastery of ambush was unparalleled within the known galaxy. Their vessels lurked, invisible to the naked eye at this distance, and cooled down to avoid sensor detection. From as far as a hundred thousand kilometers away they fired pre-charged banks of laser batteries, slicing metal and composite before closing to finish the work. The Malagath Prince knew the ships, knew the face of their commander, and knew the battle would not end with his retreat. Dirregaunt considered themselves the greatest of predators, and they would pursue him across the stars.

His helmsman said something, a buzz in his ears as a series of smaller explosions on the screen represented the remaining fighters being cut down by high-wavelength lasers. He lifted a blue, three-fingered hand to the helmsman and the remaining screens blurred as the *Dreadstar's* emergency engine fired, jumping the envoy frigate with her few survivors. His convoy died to provide him time to plot the calculations and activate the engine, generating a mass field outside the ship substantial enough to initiate a space-tear. It was the last jump the *Dreadstar* would ever make. Almost all her engineers were dead and her engines lay damaged beyond repair. His fate and the fate of his crew now rested with whomever chanced upon his distress signal. He prayed to the first stars it would not be Best Wishes.

On the bridge of the *Springdawn,* commander Best Wishes tapped his claws together with a mixture of consternation and elation. Technically, he had failed his mission objective. The *Dreadstar* fled, despite several large holes in her hull. The emergency engine was a new addition for which he had not been briefed and it allowed for a space fold to carry the Dreadstar away from battle. Rather than an easy pursuit, Best Wishes would be forced to extrapolate his trajectory based on space-time distortions his sensors read from the emergency engine. But once he followed, he would find the *Dreadstar* hanging limp. The severity of the hull compromises would cause compression shear should the First Prince attempt to accelerate past light speed, leaving the *Dreadstar* stranded wherever they emerged. A failed objective, but an opportunity to continue the hunt.

Best Wishes did not consider himself bloodthirsty. Rather, he carried a grudging respect for the Malagath and relished the opportunity to test himself further. Respect for their military prowess, if not their ideals. The Malagath culture was brutal and cruel and self-serving, antithetical to Dirregaunt philosophies. Few had more blood on their hands than the Malagath royal family, and the First Prince was the architect of several notable Dirregaunt defeats.

He considered for a moment. His ships had not gone unscathed by the exchange. For whatever else they were, the Malagath were excellent fighters. They managed to destroy two of his frigates and cripple one of his battleships, extrapolating their positions even under fire and lancing them with particle cannons before the Dirregaunt ships began to move.

"Master hailman," he said, "I do not believe we require an entire battle group to pursue a single crippled frigate. Signal the *Surf* and the *High Rain* to return to the staging station."

He turned to his first officer, Modest Bearing, who had been with his command for almost as long as he'd *had* a command. "I should like the science team working immediately. Determine where the First Prince has gone, then plot a route," he ordered. His will carried out, he turned his four eyes back to the viewport where the exhaust residue of the *Dreadstar's* emergency engine expanded in an icy cloud at the edge of their magnification.

"You cannot run from me, First Prince."

CHAPTER 1
VICK'S VULTURES

T HE *CONDOR* PUSHED AWAY from the derelict hulk. There was little of value left aboard the *Morning Spear*, but the Vultures stole it anyway. It was what they called a cold wreck. No signs of life, no hot reactor, and not one of the Big Three. Malagath, Dirregaunt, Kossovoldt; those were the name of the game. Lately, Captain Victoria Marin of the Union Earth Privateers had run as cold as that salvaged wreck tilting out of her ship's forward monitors. Six weeks without good salvage would put her command in the red right fast. Trouble was, word across the Orion Spur said there had been no recent battles between the Big Three or their proxies anywhere within range of her little puddle jumper.

Odd that, since she was in a rough part of the galaxy. Hell, all of humanity was. Earth sat practically dead center in the Orion Spur, a no-man's land providing a bridge of stars directly between the frontiers of the Malagath and Dirregaunt pushing in from the Perseus Arm and the Kossovoldt from the Sagittarius Arm towards the Galactic Core. Right where she would expect them to be fighting. She wouldn't encounter Kossovoldt in this area, a species so prominent that the local galaxy had based a common language off their influence, but the Malagath Empire and

Dirregaunt Praetory? You could hardly pull them away from each other's throats in this neck of the woods. They hated each other so much that they rarely left anything big enough to salvage anyway. Half their ships had been in service since before humans put a probe in space, but even the scrap was more valuable than her beloved *Condor*. Yet . . . no battles. Something was going on.

Victoria turned to her navigation officer.

"Huian, take us out of here. Growl Red while you're at it and have him report to the wheelhouse. He better have good news."

"Aye Skipper," said Lieutenant Wong. Victoria scowled behind the young Chinese woman's back as she stood from the captain's chair. Little blue-water puke up-jumped to space duty for being someone's daughter. Nothing against the little shit personally, but Victoria hated her rosters being mucked by political pull. Space was dangerous enough without the added variable of political nepotism.

Ducking through the hatch from the conn she made her way down two ladders, swinging past the galley and entering the officer's mess under the hand carved wooden plaque, labeling the compartment 'The Wheelhouse'. Once inside she made a beeline for the wet stores, snagging a tumbler from the wall on her way. Christ she needed this. As she was pouring the whiskey she heard the swish of the magnetic seal behind her and smelled a body recently freed from an extended vacuum suit vacation. She turned to Red Calhoun, the commander of her marines, still in his armored vacuum suit.

"Christ, Red, you could have at least dressed down. Drink with me."

The big Scotsman squeezed around the table grabbing a glass for himself. "Orders were to report to the wardroom,

Vick. 'Sides, I dress down and it gives you an excuse to stare at my ass."

Victoria scoffed, "Don't kid yourself. I've seen what you're pushing. I wouldn't write home about it," she said.

Not entirely true, the marine had good broad shoulders and strong calloused hands. And combat experience was always a plus when serving a tour in her bunk. Not that she would ever tell any of this to Red.

"Anyway," she continued, pouring a few fingers into the second glass, "Anything good?"

There was a static sensation in the air and a change in the tone of the reactor as the *Condor* slid into the super-luminal compression of her FTL drives. Outside, the ship began to move back towards the system's star for a horizon jump. Large space-time distortions were needed to enter a horizon jump. The closer to a star, the easier it became. Getting out was another matter, more of an art than a science. The hairs on Victoria's arms stood up, as they had every FTL slide since she had first climbed aboard an interstellar ship. It made her feel chilly, though every doctor she'd seen said it was psychosomatic.

Red washed his throat before answering. "A few high-freq conduits, burnt out core and storage matrixes, identification and effects of a few of the floaters and a functioning UV spectrum laser. Third generation, Tallidox made. Reactor was scuttled, but Aesop pulled some incomplete logs and schematics off a drive. Kid's a wizard with xenotech."

"In other words, garbage," she said.

"In other words . . ." said Red, nodding slowly to himself. Victoria sighed, "You know what happens if we can't haul in any decent thieving."

"I know, I know. We get to Taru station without collateral and no one will extend us more credit. Ship gets stranded and we have to wait for the *Huxley* to pay down our debt and lend us some fuel."

"And you know I hate owing Jax shit. That cocksucker and his three missing teeth still haven't let me hear the end of it from last time. Never mind when we hauled his ass out of the fire after he got those Graylings on his wake. Don't take to being ransomed, Graylings."

Red chuckled over his glass, "You remember when we pulled him outta what was left of the *Dolphin*? He was grinning so wide I thought his face'd get stuck like that. What'd he get on that haul?"

"Shit, that was the run he made off with the undamaged core manifold what let the third gen Kosso hulks push past 120c wasn't it? Old tech to them, almost ancient really, but we're still figuring it out Earth-side. That's why they gave him the *Huxley*. Shit, 120 times the speed of light? We do that, and we'll be hopping between stars in just a couple days. Without a horizon drive. We're going to go from 40 worlds to 400 before the xenos can blink. Let's see 'em try to push us out of the Orion Spur then."

"That's still a long way off, Vick. How about we start with making it back to human space?"

The two sat in silence for a time before it was interrupted by the mechanical chirp of the growler. Vick picked up the analogue receiver. Ancient tech even so far as humans were concerned, sound powered and nigh infallible the privateer fleet still made use of them for internal communications.

"Wheelhouse, Captain speaking."

"Wheelhouse sensors, Ma'am. We're getting a deliberate distress signal. Encrypted but it's a Malagath Codec. The crypto computer broke it down enough for a location. It's within Horizon range, three rungs up on the azimuth and almost on the way to Taru. Could even be hot, origin is two days old maybe."

"Shit Avery, that's Big Three, why'd you wait so long to tell me?"

"Wanted to confirm it first, Vick. I'll go ahead and kick it over to Huian."

Victoria slammed down the receiver and opened up the command network console in her retinal implants. She watched excitedly as Huian received the information and made the necessary course adjustments to change their Horizon drive destination. She stood up to activate the main circuit and address the crew but found Red had already done it for her, smiling his wide, toothy smile.

"This is the Captain." She grinned back.

"At 1900 hours we detected a distress call within horizon range. It's Big Three, people, maybe even hot. We'll be activating the horizon drive at 2050 hours. General quarters will be at 0230 hours. You know what this means. Rest up if you're not on watch, all drills are on hold. Marin out."

The cheer from the crew was audible through the metal hull of the *Condor* and Victoria couldn't help feeling proud. Even if the cheers were as much for the cancelled damage control drills as for the prospect of hot salvage. Her Vultures were the best privateers in deep space as far as she was concerned. And damn if Earth wasn't getting awful tiny in the rear-view mirror all the way out here.

"Red, you gonna get some sleep before GQ?"

He raised an eyebrow, "You?"

"Now? Shit no. I just hope no one beats us there."

"And I need to debrief my marines, and then brief them back up again, and find time for a shower in there somewhere."

In her current mood Victoria wouldn't mind debriefing

one of his marines personally. "Malagath Imperials, what can we expect if there are survivors?" she asked.

"Well if the ship is in good shape we're looking at a tactical Alcubierre drive, high density particle cannons, gravitic seekers."

"Shit. If they were in good shape there'd be no distress call."

"I agree. We manage to board, it gets a little simpler. Toxic atmo is likely, but meaningless to a marine in a vac suit. We're looking at masers and little to no tactical discipline. They haven't had an infantry battle in centuries. The ablative plates should do for the marines and I doubt the Malagath have seen a slug rifle since they went to space."

It was probably true, when humanity first entered the galactic arena they found it packed to the rafters with over a hundred other races; all at uneasy odds with each other, and none of whom still used kinetic weaponry. By and large most had made it about as far as the musket before weaponizing light, heat, accelerated particles, or radiation. Battery and energy production technologies in the galaxy-at-large were an area in which Earth struggled to catch up.

So, now she was headed toward a hulk manned by one of the Big Three. She considered the potential salvage, tapping her fingers on her tumbler. No telling what the Union Earth would do to get their hands on that tech. Or for that matter, what some of the local players might do to keep it out of U.E. hands. Red picked up his helmet and left, leaving her alone with the whiskey. She poured herself another.

—

Best Wishes examined the data brought to him by the science team. For three days they circled the departure point of the *Dreadstar*, attempting to extrapolate the trajectory and likely emergence destinations with what little they knew of the *Dreadstar's* emergency engine. High math. Nigh impossible, he would have thought, but his science team was unparalleled. He thanked the master astrotician and gave the order to his navigator. The *Springdawn* lurched into action, accelerating back towards the distant pinprick of the local star at almost 250 times the speed of light. Best Wishes did not have access to the single-use gravitic generator of the *Dreadstar's* emergency engine. They would have to use the gravity field of the red dwarf to pounce across the stars towards his prey. But he had the scent. It was only a matter of hours now. The Malagath ship fled further in a single jump than the span of most of the lesser empires, but the *Springdawn* could match it. They were both far from any allies.

First Prince Tavram huddled in the cold interior of the *Dreadstar* bridge with the nine remaining crew of his original fifty. Habitation control was a luxury they could not afford while emergency power dwindled. The hull breaches exposed the interior of the vessel to the chill of deep space, and with the reactor offline no waste heat was being produced to replace what was lost. Entropy might kill them before ever Best Wishes determined which way they had fled.

"My Prince," a ragged voice called from the sensor display. Tavram turned toward his youngest crewmember, Aurea, a female of only twenty solar cycles. His junior engineer, now his senior engineer. She looked up at him, face illuminated by the display, "A ship has entered the system, it is accelerating towards us."

"Is it the *Springdawn?* Send a signal, let us be done with

this one way or another."

"No my prince, it is moving too slowly, I cannot believe it is Dirregaunt. And I am getting very little data, nothing further than confirming that there is something coming. They should be on the optical now but even visually there is nothing."

"Sending the distress call again, short range," another voice rasped. His impromptu communicator. Previously his ship's cook. Everyone's voice was labored; carbons were building up in the ship's atmosphere. Tavram pulled up the optics display on his own console, tuning it to the proper bearing. Aurea had been right, there was nothing. At this range . . . wait, there. A star winked out. Another followed shortly, and then another along the same vector. Soon a profile began to emerge. The ship was matte black, like nothing he recognized. Had they been purposefully flying *between* stars to prevent a visual cue? A predatory tactic. The folds of skin on Tavram's slender throat began to grow moist as the ship's profile hardened. A primal reaction. Fear? No. Caution. Wariness of the unknown.

It was small, perhaps half the size of the *Dreadstar*. Odd lines. No elegance. An ugly craft. He couldn't place it with any of the lesser empires he was familiar with.

In a matter of minutes, the alien ship pulled alongside the *Dreadstar*. While obviously slow to transit, her helmsman handled her beautifully, matching the *Dreadstar's* unstable spin with maneuvering engines. Tavram wondered what the newcomers used to perform the maneuver. Some sort of gravitic adjustors? Subspace repulsors?

The *Dreadstar* jolted with a metallic thump and a spike in the passive electromagnetic sensors. Magnetic locks. Primitive, inefficient, but effective. Two more impacts resonated through the hull and the ship began to vibrate as the view through the forward monitors slowly ceased spinning. Now what? Would they tow the *Dreadstar* back to the system's core and attempt a joined space tear?

He was still postulating when a new sound came from the hull, one that could be mistaken for nothing else. *Footsteps.* Several of the remaining crew looked panicked, and even Tavram sucked in a breath of stale air. *Space walkers,* children's tales to frighten cadets. Creatures who crossed the vacuum to steal souls, who walked in the void. No, this was just an unfamiliar lesser empire, using primitive technology. It must not be . . .

"My prince, the sunward habitat chamber near the foremost hull breach has been . . . compromised. The seal has been forced open, atmosphere is venting."

"By the first stars," uttered a voice.

"Quiet," Tavram ordered. He pulled up the airlock status on his console. The venting had ceased. Had the stress on the ship from the docking caused it? Plausible. The chamber was isolated, in full vacuum now.

The icon for the inner habitation chamber hatch began to flash on his screen. Mechanical failure. *First stars, the spacewalkers were in the ship!* And he could do nothing as he tracked their progress. Nothing except buy himself a few more seconds. He ordered the survivors into position, interposing them between himself and the door. They had no weapons, but they might serve to distract while he got a few shots off. His heart raced, the cartilage in his joints expanded. These were ancient fight-or-flight traits encoded in his genome he'd not felt in years.

Even deathly thin as the atmosphere was, his entire crew's labored breathing was silent. Metallic sounds from the other side of the bulkhead were translating through the metal floor. Tavram could feel the vibrations of the spacewalkers. He fingered the single handheld maser kept on the bridge, and raised it in a ready stance. It was heavy in his hands, burdened with the weight of his lineage's survival. It wouldn't do much good against a serious enemy but the polymer grip was comforting.

Two metal prongs slid through the join in the hatch, startling a cry of alarm from his remaining crew. A mechanical whir, then the prongs began to pry the door open. The device forcing the door open was pulled away. Behind it stood several short, stocky figures. They were matte black like the alien ship had been, except for plating lining their chests and shoulders that was just slightly glossy. Two arms, two legs as evolution had produced on countless worlds as a most efficient design. In their hands they held their primitive xeno weaponry. Long, black, and slim he could not tell if it was some kind of maser like the one he had leveled or perhaps a particle beam. The array of soldiers spread into the room, fingers kept off what must be triggers for the moment. Two of the alien weapons were pointed at him while the rest scanned across his crew looking for additional threats. They found none. Their movement was martial, economical, and precise. No motion was wasted, no part of the bridge unchecked.

Tavram stared through the shaking optics of his maser at what he thought was the leader, but in truth all eight looked identical. A veteran of several space engagements, he had yet to fire a personal weapon at anyone in his life. As he looked down the gaping tunnel of that alien's weapon he did the only thing he could think to do for any hope of survival. He lowered the maser.

The change in the space walkers was instantaneous. Their deadly muzzles on their weapons lowered, their posture more relaxed, if still tight. The tallest of them reached out and took the maser from his hand. He didn't resist.

"Is there a leader among you?" he asked. The largest stepped forward.

"I am Major Red Calhoun, of the *Condor.*"

It spoke in Malagath. His voice was tinny, mechanical, unexpected. Tavram had asked in the common Kossovoldt language, but the alien had answered in his own dialect.

"Space walkers!" cried the engineer from behind Tavram, less in terror and more in amazement. He silenced her with a wave. The First Prince switched back to Malagath.

"What is your empire?" he demanded. Red? Did they often name their warriors after visible spectrum light?

"We are human," it said. Curious. Tavram had never heard of humans, but then he rarely concerned himself with the affairs of the lesser empires. After all, they were little better than animals, and over 1500 had been encountered. Some of them had even been scoured away by the Malagath. Had the emergency engine cause the *Dreadstar to* invade their space? Surely their primitive vessels could not secure a large place in the stars.

"And your intent?" asked Tavram.

The creature turned its head away, muffled sound came through the helmet, perhaps he was communicating over a shortwave communicator.

He turned back, "Our intent is to salvage mechanical technology from your ship, then take your remaining crew aboard the *Condor.*" he said.

This was met with wails of anguish behind him, and the creature raised a hand in what he must have thought was a placating gesture. "After which, we intend to return you unharmed to your people, in exchange for what supplies and technology we can barter for you. You will not be harmed in our custody."

Tavram relaxed. He had heard about outfits such as these from the lesser empires. Scavengers who picked the bones of the great battles in hopes of finding any functioning wreckage. Likely these space walkers intended to take anything valuable back to the planet Human to study. Though most were not interested in dealing with survivors, and tended to wait until there were none to move in. Some were even less interested in waiting than others.

"In the interest of self-preservation, human Red, I must inform you that we are being hunted, a Dirregaunt specialist has been tasked with eliminating this ship."

The alien quickly bobbed his head a single time. Curious gesture. "We don't plan to stay long once we get your people aboard. What is the most valuable asset aboard this ship that we can easily remove?"

The first prince gestured to himself, "You are speaking with him, human Red."

———

In the dark between stars, the *Springdawn* flew bereft of all light. More than half-way through the horizon jump they detected the superluminal distress call carrying Malagath encryption. They couldn't read it, but out this far there was little doubt what it could be. The *Dreadstar* was in truly dire straits. His science team's calculations had been almost perfect; on a stellar scale it was practically next door to their intended destination. Best Wishes complimented his astroticians and set the instructions for the next leg of their journey. Now with the distress signal's origin they could pinpoint the *Dreadstar's* location to within a few thousand meters and emerge from the second horizon jump with the laser capacitors already charged. Foolish to give themselves away.

———

"Detach the coupling here, Human Aesop. I am sorry there is so little functioning salvage for your crew."

She spoke in the lilting and fluttery tones of the Malagath language, an approximate translation relayed to Aesop's retinal implants. It was hard to believe she belonged to one of the most dangerous species in space, or that she probably viewed him as barely alive. Most species avoided contact with the Malagath where possible, they had a reputation for amorality that made most starfaring species nervous. Or dead.

The Malagath technician was wearing one of the vacuum suits the Vultures unpacked for taller humanoid rescues. It still looked uncomfortable, short and wide on her, but she quickly adjusted to the novelty of working in the vacuum of space. She still showed the fear her compatriots had during the transit to the *Condor*, but at least she was shielded from the intense black expanse her people so feared.

Aesop depressed the spots she directed and the fusion coupling separated from the reaction train, or at least what he thought was the reaction train. This ship was so advanced he barely recognized anything. His retinal implants were going nuts trying to scan and label it all, interfacing with the computer on his vacuum suit, it in turn networking with the *Condor*. He pulled the coupling from a larger piece he would have loved to tear out, but would have to cut a larger gap in the hull to carry it away. Most of it had holes anyway, which didn't help matters much. Even damaged, any engine parts were going to be e extremely valuable to Union Earth researchers, but the entire drive had been shot to hell by the Dirregaunt ambush. He passed the coupling to Aurea who pushed it through the hull breach to their waiting skiff.

He'd take this ship apart bolt by bolt if the Old Lady would let him. The captain of what he'd learned was named the *Dreadstar* insisted they leave immediately for Malagath space. Captain Marin insisted otherwise. Refugees were well and good, but they needed cold hard salvage to get enough credit at one of the neutral stations to refuel in order to get the new tech to friendly space.

His radio beeped in his ear, retinal display showing the captain's override circuit. He winced. It looked like his fun was over.

"Cohen, I just had a parley with their captain. He's made a compelling case for not being here any longer. Take what you've got and get your ass back to the *Condor*."

"Are you sure, Captain? There's still a lot of tech here I can pry loose." The line clicked dead. Not one to repeat herself, Captain Marin. He growled into his helmet before switching back to the frequency he shared with the Malagath technician.

"Aurea, they want us back on the *Condor*. We need to go now."

The tech slid a hand over the surface of the reactor shell, looking at it with an unreadable expression. Her facial expressions were unfamiliar to him, but her body language was all too recognizable. She regretted having to leave the ship that had been her home. Aesop could sympathize; he'd had a ship shot out from under him before he'd been chartered onto the *Condor*. The Orion Spur was not a friendly place, especially for species behind the technological power curve.

He followed her to the breach in the hull, bouncing

as the charge in the gravity floor plating had almost completely abated. He would have loved to pry those out and take one or two but there wasn't time. The plates were likely more efficient energy-wise to the stolen tech the *Condor* was using to generate her own artificial gravity and inertial compensation field.

Aurea reached the breach and then stopped.

"What's wrong?"

"I am . . . still nervous," she admitted, "I see the skiff, but I cannot make myself go to it."

Cohen checked on the ship's status with his retinal implants. The *Condor* was going through its Zero-G checklist, which meant he had to get back and strap down all the new salvage as well as the skiff. "Look, we don't have time for this. Just hold on to me and I'll take us over, ok?"

The tech switched places with him, wrapping her long fingers around his shoulders. The gloves of the suit fit her well. They were a plastic polymer that shrunk to form-fit whatever size hand was in them for maximum dexterity, albeit with two extra fingers the Malagath did not need. Her added mass was almost nothing as he maneuvered through the hole in the outer plating. The skiff waited just beyond, and behind it, the open bay of the *Condor*. He gently pushed off, feeling Aurea tense up against his back, but she did not cry out. He reached out for the skiff, transferring his momentum to it and making small adjustments with the thrusters to get them back in the bay. The bay door slid shut as he was barely through and the hum of the sublight engines greeted him as the ship immediately began to accelerate. The old lady must have a powerful need to be gone.

Gravity gradually returned to the bay, and Aesop was able to coax Aurea down off his back, still surprised by how light she was. He supposed he shouldn't be. Many of the races they came across were adapted to life in space with less need for physical strength and stamina, relying on their technology to do everything for them.

"There, that wasn't so bad, right?" he asked, locking down the skiff and securing netting around the cargo.

"It was . . . something I never thought I would do. It was frightening, but exciting. You humans, you do this sort of thing often? Space walking?"

"All the time, Aurea. Every ship we come across, or any time we need to make repairs on the hull. Come on, I'll show you something you might like a little better. Would you like to see the engine room?"

First Prince Tavram entered the alien ship's bridge behind her captain. A mask had been fitted over his mouth by the resident doctor to keep the oxygen from entering his respiratory system. That these creatures *required* the toxic, flammable gas to survive had flabbergasted him. It seemed the more he learned about this strange little race the more mystery lay ahead. They were clearly matriarchal, aligned behind this captain who asserted dominance by baring her teeth at each crewmember she passed, each of whom returned the gesture in kind. They breathed poison, walked in space, greeted each other with threats, and each member of the crew could perfectly understand his language, though most could not speak it and used the lesser Kossovoldt tongue instead when speaking to him and each other. Baffling. He had asked about human language, and learned it was largely tribal and that many of her crew did not speak a common human language.

The 'ship' as they called it, was primitive. Simple forged

steel construction with obvious joining of different metals and outdated composites. Wires and piping snaked everywhere like thick vines, carrying power, potables, and hydraulic fluids. But it was still ingenious in a barbaric sort of way.

"Captain Ma'am, Sergeant Cohen is aboard and we're on our way as ordered."

"Good, hold steady, max acceleration. Build us up some speed, I have a bad feeling. How's the trajectory for a horizon shot?"

"Nav computer has it locked in steady with the star's gravity. We'll have broken line of sight with the *Dreadstar* when we make the jump. We'll need one more star before we can hit Taru station. ETA to jump five two minutes."

Nav computer? Who would trust such delicate computations to a computer? Were they jumping one star at a time? Perhaps these humans with their primitive brains were more limited than he thought. After all, they had only been among the stars for the last hour of the Malagath Empire. According to their captain, anyway. There was much she had been reluctant to discuss. From his forced crouch he could see the navigation monitor, though the numerals on it weren't Kosso standard. Not much to be learned there. There was a third seat in the command center of the *Condor*, marked with a cross and a circle. He took it, his knees somewhere by his shoulder made for an uncomfortable position, though better than hunching beneath the low ceiling.

"Control, sensors. Photon Doppler detected, superluminal contact bearing relative one-eight-zero, one-four degrees azimuthal out of the horizon."

"Sensors, conn aye. Shit that was quick. Yuri, you get all that? Shutter the drives, turn on the GSD." The captain flicked a switch, turning the open receiver to the main circuit, "This is the Captain speaking. A superluminal contact has been detected, we are engaging the gravitic stealth device and going ballistic. Stow for Zero-G," she turned to Tavram, "You're going to be floating here in a second, chief. Strap into that stay."

The subtle shuddering of the ship ceased as the engines were shut down. Their constant hum was replaced by a new oscillation, a strengthening of the artificial gravity drive, he thought. His weight began to lessen, and he attached the lanyard the captain had pointed out. He still felt slightly panicky and, though he would never admit it, somewhat sick. Malagath artificial gravity could be localized practically to square meters

"Full ballistic, ma'am,"

"Good, bring up the *Dreadstar* on the main screen."

"Aye ma'am."

"I do not understand, human Victoria. We are simply flying in a straight line in hopes he will not see us?"

"Not now, chief. When we're out of it." She replied. Tavram chafed at being addressed so by this lesser empire captain. Her tiny ship barely had room for her ego, it seemed. And yet she had saved his life at risk to her own. This 'privateer' as she had called it, who knew the value and safety of a rescued spacefarer. Pragmatic? Astoundingly so, and reasonable if rigid. Martial yet disciplined. Primitive yet, well, resourceful. The rational side of him looked forward to learning more about them on the trip back to the Malagath Empire. If they survived the next few minutes, at any rate. Unlikely, as they would be picked up in the first round of the *Springdawn*'s active sensors.

The *Dreadstar* appeared on the monitors and Tavram's neck folds moistened, a reaction of the increased blood flow and body temperature. *Such detail.* It was as if his broken and battered ship were still abreast of the *Condor*.

"Control, sensors. Here she comes, Vick."

"Thanks Avery. Steady on course, Huian."

Again Tavram was impressed, until he remembered that the *Condor* had probably stolen the superluminal sensor technology from another empire. The view screen though, he knew of no one who could produce such optics resolution. Where had they found that?

"Ok people, hold on to your asses."

There was silence but for the hum of the anti-gravity device. On the screen, hundreds of thousands of kilometers away, a second, *massive* ship winked out of horizon space less than 100 meters from the *Dreadstar*, dwarfing it. The sleek lines and narrow profile of the *Springdawn* was unmistakable, as was the skill of her navigation team. There was a warning from sensors of energy weapon signature, and Commander Best Wishes unleashed his high-wavelength lasers at point blank range. Though the lasers fell outside his visible spectrum their effect on his ship was all too obvious. The metal burned, twisted, and flew apart under their fire. Again and again the lasers cut, pulverizing any section larger than a few meters into space slag. Tavram couldn't stop himself from keening. It was as though his heart was being pierced by the *Springdawn*'s fire. Even at this range, the lasers interfered with the optics of the *Condor*, causing the screen to flash when they fired.

The reactor shielding was breached, though the explosion only harmlessly scattered the remains of his beloved *Dreadstar.*

The captain turned to him, "You're sure he'll ping us?" she asked.

Tavram nodded, attempting to compose himself, "He

will. He is thorough, and will take no chances. I am surprised he has not seen the heat signature of your ship already."

The captain didn't answer him, instead thumbing the main circuit again.

"This is the Captain. As of 0430 hours the *Dreadstar* has been destroyed by a hostile Dirregaunt cruiser designated Primary. We are expecting an active sensor pulse imminently. The attenuator is online. It's going to get a bit warm."

Sure enough the sensors called it out just as the electromagnetic wave passed over them.

"Captain, nine-nine point five percent attenuation. Pulse strength recorded at . . . oh God, 1.2 gigawatts."

"Fuck, Yuri shut down the attenuator now! If we eat another pulse we'll all be boiled."

A wave of heat washed over control and Tavram gasped. Instantly the room had become an oven, the metal rail which he gripped painful to touch. He could see heat shimmers in the air, and every light and screen began to flicker. What happened?

"Engineering, conn. Come in. Engineering, conn. Shit," the captain thumbed the general circuit, "Damage control parties to engineering."

CHAPTER 2
ATTENUATION

Sergeant Aesop Cohen sucked scalding fire into his lungs. At least that's what it felt like. Beside him, Aurea hung weightless attempting not to touch any of the scalding hot metal that surrounded them as she roused him. He hadn't felt heat like this since fighting a fire aboard the *Hyperion*. Thank god the vacuum suit still protected most of his body or he'd be in as bad a shape as the other engineers. They floated at the ends of their lanyards, passed out or worse. Most of engineering was down, both equipment and personnel, and the heat sirens were blaring in his ears. Who knew what damage to the computers the heat had done before they'd automatically shut down. The smell of burnt circuitry was heavy in the air. Faint blue smoke drifted in the dark compartment, illuminated by sporadic flashes from the struggling lights.

"Human Aesop, what is going on?"

He coughed, his throat so dry and rough he could barely speak, "The attenuator. It turns the electromagnetic energy of active sensors into heat energy and disburses it inside the ship. It stops a reflection, but we have to deal with the waste heat."

"There are no safeguards against this?" asked Aurea, gesturing around them at the smoking equipment.

"We don't have data on Dirregaunt sensors, 1.2 giga-watts is 10 times the *Condor's* peak output. Just for an active sensor sweep? Come on."

Aesop detached his lanyard and pushed towards the upper deck of engineering.

"Human Aesop, your comrades!"

"We have to shut down the attenuator first. If they pulse again we won't survive the temperature increase."

The heat on the upper level was even worse. Aesop pushed past the free-floating form of Chief Engineer Denisov, stopped briefly to check his pulse to make certain Yuri was still alive before continuing towards the firefighting locker. He winced as the latches singed his bare hands, having stowed his gloves and helmet before showing Aurea the engine room. He pulled out two pairs of asbestos gloves, handing one to Aurea. She seemed better able to handle the heat, but she tugged them on anyway, filling only the first two fingers and thumb of each glove.

Pushing himself toward the attenuator he could see shimmering air coming off the device's vents. It looked fried, but it was built to work at extreme temperatures. "Aurea," he called, trying to ignore the feeling of his face baking as he drew closer. It was like sticking his face into an oven. "Those cables on the other side are where it interfaces with the matte plating on the hull. When I give you the signal, pull them out. There will be sparks."

Aesop tore open the fore panel. Smoke billowed out, along with the acrid stench of burned rubber. The gaskets and fan bearings had melted. It was easy to see why, much of the shielding for the cables within had melted together too. Coughing, he plunged his hand in up to the shoulder, trying to keep his cheek from touching the top of the panel. He felt around, looking for the emergency shutoff he knew was there. His finger wrapped around the little lever and he jerked it forward, hoping the innards of the device hadn't been completely slagged.

The lever cut power to the attenuator from the engine room, but after absorbing a pulse it could self-power for a time off the waste heat, enough to trigger the reactive plating on the hull. Even after shutting it down it was still a danger while hardwired to the plating, but pulling those connections without securing power first would almost certainly start a fire. The lever isolated the attenuator from the ship's reactor, but the device was still able to self-power from waste heat. The only problem was, any more heat would lead to a fire. Fire killed a ship as dead as any xeno weapon. The *Ulysses,* the *Merit,* and the *Haldeman* had all been lost to shipboard fires. A fire in space doubled in size every 30 seconds and a closed system left nowhere for the smoke to go unless the captain vented the entire atmosphere. It took less than 5 minutes to choke everyone aboard those ships and raise the cabin temperature over 200 degrees Celsius.

"Aurea, now!" he shouted. She braced her feet against the bulkhead, screaming as the heat from the metal burned her right through the thin shoes of her suit. She yanked at the cables, putting the leverage offered by her long legs to use. The thick cords resisted briefly, then snapped free in a shower of sparks. No longer held in place by the tension of the cables, the Malagath technician spun across the engine room, slamming against the bulkhead with a sickening crunch. On the level below he heard the access hatch to the central compartment open and the damage control teams enter the engine room to search for fires and casualties.

Aurea collided with a backup engineering console and was now drifting nearby. He pushed off the attenuator, reassuring her as he moved to thumb the control circuit.

"Bridge engineering, attenuator offline and disconnected."

The captain's voice, previously issuing orders to the damage control station switched back to the open microphone, "Engineering bridge aye, what's your status?"

"Lieutenant Denisov is down, along with the rest of engineering. Lots of burns. No fires that I can see but most of the equipment is offline. Captain, without the attenuator we're naked, another sweep will spot us."

"You let me worry about the fucking sensor sweeps, right? You get your ass to the GSD and keep that fucker online. And stay out of damage control's way if you can. If there's no fire we'll circulate the engine room, get some cool air in there at least. We can't vent in view of that battleship," said Captain Marin. True to her word, the fans began to hiss, blowing blessedly cool air into the compartment. It was a temporary relief; the ship was only going to get hotter until they could break line of sight with the Dirregaunt ship.

Aurea whimpered beside the console, "I believe my shoulder has broken. But I will help if I can."

"No, you need to get to DC central and get that looked at."

"By what doctor? Is your medic versed in Malagath physiology? I am staying."

He cursed, but she was right. The doc would have no idea how to treat her. "Alright follow me," he said. He pushed off towards the aft ladder. The gravitic stealth device was on the fore end of the second level, but taking the aft ladder would keep him out of damage control's way. As he pulled himself down the rungs he saw two crewmembers in firefighting gear floating unconscious engineers back toward the hatch.

"Aesop, where the hell you going?"

"The GSD," he called back, "It goes offline and that cruiser will spot us whether or not it does another active sweep." He shouted back.

"Get going then, boy. You waiting on an invitation?"

Aurea followed closely behind. Nearing the hatch, he swung left to get out of another pair's way, then bounced to the GSD. The gravitic stealth device wasn't anything to write home about. No flashing lights, no soft green glow. It was based on tech they stole from the Havash, an amphibious race who developed it to help their ships fly like something other than huge tanks of water. The Havash had adapted it from the Kreesvay, who had stolen it from someone else. On the *Condor*, it analyzed her mass' pull on space-time down to the kilogram and pumped out an equivalent antigravity field. It took a lot of power, and wouldn't work at the same time as the artificial gravity generator so they couldn't make major acceleration changes while using it. But many hostile xenos used gravitic field analysis in their passive sensor suites, and the GSD hid them from that. After leaving the Mossad, Aesop got his degree in xeno-technology, and had always been shocked at how little the rest of the galaxy had developed stealth warfare. Even the Dirregaunt, who loved ambush tactics, made no effort to remain hidden once battle was joined.

Then again, he reflected as he pulled up the diagnostic panel on the GSD, *the ones who are good at it, we don't know about.*

The LCD display was completely cooked, but the device was humming so it hadn't shut down yet. It had independent heat sinks to deal with the extra waste heat it generated and that's where the danger lay. Aesop grabbed the diagnostic tool, plugging it into the port of one cooling tower, then the other.

"Shit. Aurea, this thing needs new heat sinks, it's getting close to burning out. That case there," he said, pointing. The Malagath technician tore open the shelf, pulling a pair of tall slender heat sinks from within and letting them drift nearby. She was adapting well to the zero-G conditions, despite her injury.

"Good, bring them over here. We'll have to do it by hand with the automatic system down. I'll show you what to do."

"I cannot change these with my broken arm, human Aesop."

"I know, I'll do that. Take this tool," he said, handing her the diagnostic reader, "when I say, hit this button here to open the shielding, and then this one to close it once the new heat sink is installed. Got it?"

"I understand," she said, taking the diagnostic tool from him.

"Press it."

The shielding slid open and the air began to hiss and shimmer as the heat sink was exposed. Because warming up the place a bit was exactly what they needed to do. If the attenuator had been an oven, this was a forge-fire ready to bake steel. Holding his breath so as not to burn his lungs he grabbed the handle on the heat sink and pulled the red-hot tower out of the GSD, glove sizzling. He let it hang in midair, out of the way for now and quickly shoved in the replacement unit. Aurea closed the shielding. He would have to move the old one to the deck before the gravity was switched back on. If it could switch back on. Hopefully having it offline protected it, otherwise they'd be limited to what acceleration the human body could tolerate, which wasn't a great deal.

"Why are they like this? Is one enough?" she asked.

Aesop shook his head, "No, the GSD is at the failsafe shutdown. Both towers need to work in tandem or we lose the gravitic field. The attenuator offloads excess heat to other heat sinks across the ship, they're probably all like this except for the main computer."

He maneuvered to the other tower and swapped the cord for the diagnostic tool, "Ok, now," he said.

The shielding slid open. He gripped the handle, tugging against the cooling tower. The heat sink barely budged. He swore, letting go of the handle as the heat began to bleed through the thick firefighting gloves. Looking around desperately he spotted the lanyard on Aurea's uniform.

"Aurea, I need your tether," he said. *Good girl,* he thought as she unhooked it and passed it to him, *didn't even ask why.*

Aesop looped the length of cord around the top of the heat sink and slid it down behind. He braced his foot against the base of the tower and heaved again. He felt something sliding and pulled even harder, rope crackling. The heat sink came free, slamming into his chest and bouncing away, missing his face by inches and leaving a shiny streak down the front of his vacuum suit. The wind was knocked from him and he spun out of control until he collided painfully with the water purifier. As fast as he was able he righted himself and shot after the heat sink to stop it from crashing into anything flammable. While he did, Aurea managed to shove the second replacement in and close the shielding with the diagnostic tool.

Aesop winced as the rogue heat sink crashed into the aft hydraulic pump, but managed to catch it before it could smash into the starboard power bus. He reached out for something and found a pipe joint. His momentum shifted direction and he slammed into what would have been the deck of the level above them, had the ship had gravity. He let the heat sink go. They had done it. Aesop began to laugh, deep, so hard it almost hurt.

"Human Aesop what is wrong, are you hurt? You're frightening me"

Aesop wiped away tears from the corner of his eye with a soot-stained finger, "No Aurea I'm not hurt. Not badly, anyway. I just can't believe we did it. Though I suppose we're not out of it yet. You were brilliant, Aurea."

"Look!" exclaimed Aurea. Aesop twisted to where she pointed in her ill-fitting glove, worried it was some new crisis. But she pointed at the lanyard, spinning slowly through the air. It was on fire from the heat of the second tower, but the flames adhered to the cord in a close sheet in an almost beautiful way. Aesop continued to laugh.

———

Victoria scowled at the muted optic image of the *Springdawn* as it began to slide around the horizon of the local star. She watched unblinking for a count of ten before speaking into the open microphone. "Yuri, we back online back there?"

"Aye Captain, still undermanned but we're good for a dump-and-jump"

"Roger that. Shutdown the gravitic stealth, flush coolant and prep the horizon drive. Oh, and give Cohen a fucking raise."

"Aye Captain."

She switched the main viewport to the forward aspect and watched the star's rotation on screen. The ship's belly banked toward the dwarf star and with the automatic cooling system back online they ejected every spent heat sink where no enemy ship could detect them. Gravity returned and she felt the signature shudder of the horizon drive warming up.

"Miss Wong," she said, looking at Huian, "Get us the fuck out of here."

"Aye Skipper."

The *Condor* used the star's gravity to pierce into horizon space, and rocketed away from the *Springdawn* and the atomized remains of the *Dreadstar*.

Best Wishes stood at the fore of the bridge, hands resting upon the bone protuberances of his chest. Before him, the view screen replayed the final moments of the *Dreadstar*. The attack had been masterful. Swift. Without warning or opportunity for reprisal, as a hunt should be. He had complimented his crew on it. But he would find room for improvement, as he always did. Every skirmish was a lesson and Best Wishes was a scholar of battle. He had to be, for a member of the lower caste who had elevated himself through merit there was no other honor to be had. His ambition would falter, he knew, when he could no longer climb. He would forever do the dirty work of the Praetory. He was doomed to command small battle groups striking from the shadows, never to strategize grand fleet movements.

"Again," he commanded, all four eyes locked on the screen. His first officer, Modest Bearing, complied with his order. Again the slippery blue-black waves of the interstellar dispersed to reveal the *Dreadstar*, and moments later the already warm weapons of the *Springdawn* began to cut her to smaller and smaller pieces. She had been so close to the point of the distress call that they had emerged not only within visual range, but so near that he could have thrown a spanner from one vessel to the other.

So why did something feel wrong?

"Again," he barked. The recording reset back to the interstellar emergence. "Hold," he said, raising his hand as the dark waves faded and the *Dreadstar* appeared. Modest Bearing stopped the recording.

First Prince Tavram's ship had been without engine power, as evidenced by her stationary position relative to the earlier distress call, and by initial readings recorded before the attack. *So then why is she perfectly oriented to the local stellar plane?* he wondered. Troubling. He turned away from the screen, "Master detector, bring me the report on the active sweep and the passive sensor analysis if you please."

The secondary view screen flickered, then displayed the result of the active sweep. Nothing of note, no space junk larger than a few inches across that was not a planet.

"Thermal," he requested. Again, nothing of note. A small flare of heat near the bearing of the sun shortly after the active sweep, but a small flare was hardly remarkable. "Now show the gravitic," came the command.

A display of the disturbances in space-time replaced the thermal readout, both real time and at the moment they had warped into the system. This was pointless, if there was anything worth his attention his sensor team would have alerted him at the time. Why did his doubt persist, despite the success of his attack?

"Spectrum." A list and analysis of elements that made up the wreckage of the *Dreadstar* appeared before him. He scanned it, unsure of what he expected to find. He stopped partway down. Ionized xenon, attributed to the *Dreadstar's* laser banks. But xenon produced lasers in the ultraviolet range, whereas Tavram's ship had lasers of a yellowing color on the visible light spectrum. Helium-Neon, if he recalled correctly. He scanned down. Sure enough, the discrepancy had been overlooked and there were two gasses attributed to the *Dreadstar's* lasers.

"Master detector, give me a bearing for the highest concentration of xenon."

The sensor officer, Dutiful Heiress, listed a series of numbers. He snuck a glance at her as she looked to her console, but one of her eyes swiveled, dispelling his attempt at subtlety.

"And the thermal discrepancy I noted previously?"

A pause, "The same, my Commander. The very same. But of the active sweep and the gravitic sensors there is nothing."

Troubling. Best Wishes tapped upon his bone protuberances in consternation. He eyed one of the junior shipmen serving as a bridge runner. Earthen Musk. Best Wishes knew the name of every member of his crew down to the last unranked child. Even the clandestine pets that were smuggled aboard. "You there, Earthen Musk," he called. The youth shriveled under the attention of his captain. Whether from nerves, or disgust at being forced to serve under one of lower caste, Best Wishes could not be sure. There was plenty of both aboard the *Springdawn* and within the battle group.

"Run to the archivist, request knowledge of any of the lower empires who use xenon in their propulsion systems." He looked to the helmsman, "Master handler, take us to the far side of the star, if you would."

Within minutes the *Springdawn* was on a smooth parabola, and as the opposite hemisphere of the local star was crested his sensor team detected a vicious tear in local space-time consistent with the interstellar ignition of less evolved drives. Inelegant but effective. So, there was a chance the first prince still lived.

"Master hailman, relay a message to the science team. We have a new destination for them."

CHAPTER 3
THE FIRST PRINCE

COMFORTABLE IN THE protection offered by interstellar travel, Victoria settled onto the bench in the Wheelhouse with a tumbler of whiskey opposite the Malagath First Prince. If this kept up, she'd have to break open her private supply before journey's end. The First Prince had to twist sideways to fit his long legs on the narrow bench, so Red had squeezed in beside her. Free space was a premium on interstellar ships and the *Condor* had not been designed with Malagath ergonomics in mind.

"We're out of the hot water for now. Before we hit Taru, I think we should continue our conversation, Tav.

The Malagath opposite her twitched. "The proper honorific to address me is First Prince."

Victoria scratched the back of her neck, "Alright, I suppose that was a bit too familiar. Didn't mean to offend your sensibilities, First Prince. What are you doing in our neck of the woods, crippled, so far from any battle we know of?"

The First Prince spread one slender hand before him on the table, "Human Victoria—"

"Captain Marin. If we're standing on titles then aboard my ship I will be addressed as such," Victoria interrupted. She grinned briefly as he recoiled at the interruption. Red kicked her under the table, but she ignored him. Big Three be damned, no one was above manners on the *Condor*. Except her.

"Very well Captain. Since you have saved the lives of myself and my crew I will offer disclosure. In return though, I would know more of your culture and your own history. In particular, how you came to be walkers of the void."

Victoria nodded, "Sounds fair. Though Red here is the history buff, so he'll probably be doing most of the talking. You realize, of course, there are things I cannot tell you, such as the location of our worlds and the disposition of our population. Even though it wouldn't change anything for you to know."

"Please explain."

Victoria gestured to him with her tumbler, "You hold so many worlds and so much territory that information propagates slowly through the empire. Policy change, technological advances, even knowledge of worlds gained and lost. Also you're so far above us technologically that we aren't even playing in the same universe. Let me give you an example. There are six instances to date of Human-Malagath contact. Every human astronaut has studied these encounters ad nauseam and entire careers have been built writing about the Malagath history, technical capabilities, fleet tactics, and logistics networks. But half the time you meet a new race you blow it out of the sky and don't even bother to write it down. Four of those instances you didn't even know we were there. We're a bug on the wall to you."

"An unfortunate shortcoming of our empire, Captain Marin. Though after watching the way you handled the *Springdawn* I would expect humans will soon become a force among the lesser empires. Truth also be told your tactics resemble legends of monsters in our past, before Malagath came to supremacy. Tales of black beings who walked in the space between ships."

Victoria stared. "In space so long even your fucking legends are about space ships. Unbelievable. But if the terms are fair, how did you come about needing to be rescued?"

"I was on my way to negotiate with the Dirregaunt Primarch. We were intending to broker a ten year truce, with hopes of perhaps a longer lasting peace between our two peoples. My father, the Emperor, was against it but gave his blessing to conduct the mission. The Lords of the Hunt urged the Primarch to deny me, but for some reason he acquiesced. It seems their loyalty was not absolute."

Red whistled, "That'd certainly be something, First Prince. You two and the Kossovoldt have been fighting since we were struggling to build barrow mounds, and a stick with a sharp rock tied to it was the pinnacle of technology."

"Indeed, human Red, it would be an occasion for the histories. The first time in millennia in which the Dirregaunt and the Malagath Empire ceased hostilities. But it is not to pass, we were betrayed from within one or both empires. The Dirregaunt dissenters knew our route and sent their deadliest commander to intercept us, likely against the wishes of the Primarch. Despite his low status, Best Wishes and the *Springdawn* are known throughout the Malagath Empire. My ship alone escaped, and he followed. He is one of the few commanders to take the oaths of servitude seriously and will only stop pursuit at the direct order of his admirals or the Primarch himself."

There was a pause as the XO's voice sounded over the main circuit, securing the *Condor* from general quarters.

"Well we've given him the slip for now," interjected Red, "scary bastard. Still, when we get to Taru Station I think it best you and your crew remain on board for the most part. If we get some privacy in the bay then at least get out and stretch your legs but it doesn't need to be getting out that we're carrying Malagath rescues. That's one hell of a storm. I'll be in charge of security, both on and off ship. We'll conduct our business, take on fuel, supplies, and repairs, and we'll also need to contact Earth."

"Earth?" the First Prince asked.

"Our home planet."

Tavram wheezed, the Malagath equivalent of a laugh. The sound slightly tinny through the breathing mask, "You call your planet Earth? Not Human? Why not simply call it dirt, or perhaps ground?"

Victoria scowled, "That's the Kosso word for it, yes, but the meaning is the same. We call it Earth because we came from it, not the other way 'round. Maybe it's easier to lose sight of that when you've been colonizing planets for 10,000 years. We wouldn't know."

"My apologies, Captain Marin, human Red. I did not mean to offend. I must admit it is uniquely humble. On Earth, you must contact your admiral?"

"Not exactly, no. Officially we're civilians. We report to the State and Colony department of the Union Earth government. The human navy is restricted to protecting Earth and her colonies. It's not allowed any outside contact with xenos unless attacked. Happened a few times, always ended bad for us. So now Union Earth maintains a fleet of privateers. Our mission is to establish human rapport in the local neighborhood and try to close the technological gap by salvaging wrecks from space battles, and in this case by transporting rescues in exchange for material rewards and good will."

"In other words, you pick the bones of dead ships clean and you steal everything you can get your hands on before someone else gets to it."

Victoria spread her hands and smiled, "The crew of the *Condor* ain't called Vick's Vultures for nothing. When we made first contact we realized how hopelessly outclassed we were in space. Now we know of almost a hundred other xenos and we're only *mostly* hopelessly outclassed by their tech. We're bottom quarter, maybe. That's where the other half of our mission comes in, establishing rapport."

She paused. The first prince gestured for her to proceed so she continued, "We try to maintain a discreet presence on most of the neutral stations we know of, either through a human office or one of our few allied xeno friends. That's how we keep the privateers supplied and sheltered in port during storms. We need a good safety net to function well. We've also established that humans will never attack on sight, and are more interested in rescue and salvage than slaughter. We place a great weight on the importance of individual life within a unit, and shame for those who put themselves above their comrades."

"Not asserting strength of arms is an excellent way to have the more predatory empires blast you from the stars, I would think."

"You'd be right, First Prince," Victoria. She looked at Red. "By all means, Major, you're the fucking marine. You field this one."

He nodded. "Sure, a lot of them don't give two shits who we are but most of the other xenos learned pretty early on not to touch us, despite our apparent disadvantages."

"Pray tell, human Red. What caused this amnesty?"

"Well to put it bluntly, disregarding our desire to avoid confrontation of arms and loss of life, and even with our limited tech, it's been clear to us from the get-go that humans are the sneakiest sons of bitches in the Orion Spur."

Victoria continued, "We thought everyone else was so

alien and it turns out we're the weirdest of the bunch. Everyone else we've met put away their differences before they launched their first satellite. But human tribes have been warring with each other our entire history, with stealth and subterfuge playing a bigger and bigger part. Hell, even our first moon landing was a type of war. As far as we can tell we're the only ones that turned atomic weapons on our own kind not just once, but three times and managed to get past it. No one wars like humans do. Our tactics, weaponry, everything is such an utter *mystery* to everyone else in the neighborhood. You saw some of that yourself. Our greatest battles were victories against overwhelming odds, and now we're more outnumbered than we've ever been."

"Indeed, even your tribalism is unique. By all accounts, species that turn nuclear weapons upon themselves fail to colonize before total destruction. But if you are so effective in combat despite your shortcomings, why avoid conflict? You must know it is faster to seize colonies with existing infrastructure than to build new ones."

"We have a saying, *If you want peace, prepare for war.* We don't fuck with anyone, nor do we tolerate being fucked with. It helps that we can only colonize worlds with heavily oxygenated atmospheres. Not many xenos seem to like those."

The first prince settled back on the bench a moment, apparently considering her words. She already told him more than she was comfortable discussing about humanity. What he would do with it she didn't know. Probably nothing, all accounts placed the Malagath Empire at almost 8,000 worlds. Once delivered, the First Prince would likely never think of her again. She had to do some consideration herself. An empire of 8,000 worlds and their second in line for the seat of emperor was on her ship. What were the odds on that? He was the hottest cargo she'd ever transported, and would bring them either ruin or fortune. She couldn't say which was more likely.

Victoria stood, "We've got a few hours before we hit Taru system. Rest if you need it. You and your crew are not confined to the passenger quarters, though I do have to make clear that I don't want them interfering with the duties of my crew. With the exception of the sensor compartment, the operations center, and the server cluster, you have the run of the ship. Hell, I heard one of your technicians is assisting with some repairs in the engine room. It is good to have you aboard, First Prince Tavram."

The first prince stood as well, considerably hunched over, "It is good to be aboard, Captain Marin, human Red. I find it very preferable to being atomized.

The *Condor* used the gravity distortion of what the locals called Taru star like a wide net to slide out of horizon space. The Vultures slipped from the blue-black irrational shapes of the interstellar corridor back into the pure dark sky somewhere outside the orbit of the fourth planet, a good clip closer to the star than her last navigator had been able to manage. Victoria grudgingly admitted that Huian was learning her business, though she'd yet to see how the girl handled herself in a fight. From outside the orbit of the fourth, the navigator stealthily made her way towards Taru station in orbit around the first. They avoided revealing their presence until almost within the planet's gravity, hailing for permission to dock with the natural satellite.

It started life as a large asteroid networked with a warren of tunnels and caverns. The Salvesei launched a massive operation to integrate airlocks, power, artificial gravity, and other infrastructure necessary to support a neutral station. Ultimately to their financial advantage, as dozens of species made Taru station a way point on their interstellar journeys for business or exploration. Docking fees, fuel, and trade tariffs were the primary sources of profit for the Salvesei, and more than offset the upkeep of the huge station.

Though the Salvesei staffed and ran the station, it was considered a truly neutral site, and outside the secured areas all visitors were responsible for their own safety once landed.

After a brief negotiation between Victoria and the docking coordinator on watch, the *Condor* landed at a private berth and the crew prepared for a rushed refit.

CHAPTER 4
TARU STATION

Victoria descended the ramp from the salvage bay airlock, ablative vest secreted beneath her jacket and sidearm strapped to her hip. The marines wore their armored vacuum suits, absent the hard shell helmet in favor of a more inconspicuous hood that could be secured on a moment's notice. Half of them would stay in the bay and guard the ship, the others would guard crew where needed.

Each crewmember had a tube running up to their nostrils, supplying the needed oxygen in an otherwise pure nitrogen environment. The nitrogen prevented most types of fires, important when xenos hurled plasma at each other. The rounds in the marine's rifles carried their own oxidizer, and could even fire in a vacuum or underwater.

Each crewmember had a tube running up to their nostrils, supplying the needed oxygen in an otherwise pure nitrogen environment. The nitrogen prevented most types of fires, important when xenos hurled plasma at each other. The rounds in the marine's rifles carried their own oxidizer, and could even fire in a vacuum or underwater.

"Alright, Cohen you take point to get whatever engineering parts from UE storage we need. I'll talk to Hibbevox and get us some credit so we can take on some food stores, coolant, and EM for the Alcubierre and horizon drive. Red, that's you, get ready to start moving it on board. After that I'll get that message routed through the Union channel. I don't like how far they put us from the square, but at least we're not sharing the damn bay."

"It seem quiet to you, Vick?" asked Red. He was sliding a gloved finger up and down the manual safety switch of his rifle.

"No, but something doesn't fucking feel right." She looked at her gathered marines. They were all in various states of alert, scanning corners and exits. "You've all got your plugs in. No one goes alone, not even to the shitter. You all know the drill."

She led the way. The halls of Taru weren't crowded this far from what most privateer crews referred to as New Times Square. What xenos they did see quickly made themselves scarce at the sight of armed humans.

"They avoiding us even more than usual, Red?" she asked. They'd come through almost a mile of pock-marked tunnels, eerily quiet aside from the rhythmic clacking of atmospheric scrubbers.

"Seems so. Almost like they know we've got hot cargo. Hell, I don't even like having them on board. They're plenty cordial now, but you know if they'd come across us they'd have blasted our ship to dust without even thinking about it."

They stopped, letting a pair of marines check around a corner before continuing. "I don't think it's that, Red. If anyone knew who our honored guests were we'd be getting fucking swarmed. Not a soul on this station what hasn't lost family to the Malagath, and not a soul wouldn't kill for that tech. No, it's something else. Like we're an unholy walking shitstorm they don't want dragging into." The tunnel began to widen, the noise of gathered voices beginning to win out over the hollow footfalls and rush of nitrogen. "Come on, the square's up ahead. At least there's security there so we can unpucker a bit."

Foot and cargo vehicle traffic increased as they entered the thoroughfare leading to New Times Square. The Salvesei had their own name for it, but the towering stone pillars honeycombed with various offices inside the cavernous space bore a striking resemblance to the American namesake. Once you discounted the materials, temperature, lack of oxygen, and thousands of bustling xenos.

"Testing, testing, one two," said Victoria, tapping the transmitter stuck to her throat by a minor adhesive. Her voice sounded in her own ear through the receiver, and to the other members of her crew. It was the second time she checked them, but damned if she wasn't feeling nervous for some reason.

"Alright," she continued, "You all know what you're about, so be about it. Anything off, you put it on the shortwaves. Red, I want two of your boys with me."

"I bet."

She snorted, but Red detached a small detail of two men to accompany her so she bit back on a retort. Shouldn't put too much pressure on his squad, he still had six with him and Sergeant Cohen had five. Odd one, that Cohen. An engineer what was also a marine. Damned if he wasn't useful though. Pleasing to look on as well, if not the flavor she usually preferred. Hands that knew their way around a wrench.

She took her detail of two marines in the direction of the closest thing they had to an ally in Taru Station, a Jenursa by the name of Hibbevox. His office moved around a lot. Jenursa were migratory by nature, shuffling about the ocean floors and marshes of their planets. They made good cohabitators with a few of the human colonies, an effort by

Union Earth to share the burden of defense.

"Let's check the fifth deck cantina, maybe he's sipping on a brine shake."

"*HUMANS.*"

Victoria froze, hand hovering over her sidearm. There was that other shoe dropping. She turned as the marines raised their rifles, safeties switching off. Security forces nearby reacted as well, and high-pitched whines filled the air as Salvesei guards primed the capacitors on their small arms. Striding toward her on six legs came a creature halfway between a rhinoceros beetle and a nightmare. It spoke in an impossibly deep hissing Kosso common, but behind it was the twisted chirp of creepy crawly. It was a Grah'lhin, or a Grayling as the humans called them. Whenever she heard it she was brought back to the summer the cicadas hatched in her home town, drowning out the rest of the world in their ear-piercing, constant choir. She motioned for her marines to lower their weapons, but she noticed the Salvesei kept theirs raised.

"Bargult, the universe hasn't flushed you down the toilet yet?" she asked.

The other xenos were again giving them a wide berth, even in the relative sanctuary of the square.

"*It has tried, human Victoria,*" said Bargult as he circled the trio, "*I am far from here. I look upon the dusted remains of a ship of the founders. You would not know of this perchance?*"

She shivered. Many bodies, one brain. Shit gave her the willies. The creature called Bargult was a singular entity spread across the crew of multiple Grayling ships operating in the area. A quantum entanglement in the nervous system of the brood networked the entire clutch with a naturally evolved FTL communication and shared sensory input. The only thing humans had encountered that came close was the ocular implant networking of each individual privateer. But individuals had delays. Individuals had to give and receive orders. Grayling communication was perfect. Like worker ants that each carried a bit of the queen inside. Kill a few and they could just hatch more. To kill a Grayling you had to stamp out the whole damn hive down to single digit population before there wasn't enough brain matter to process the Grayling consciousness.

Luckily the species as a whole had so few individuals spread across numerous bodies that creativity and development was stifled as a result. The Graylings were perhaps a century ahead of humans in the technological curve, where they stagnated even as their colonies spread.

"*Human Victoria. You have been too long from my senses. Will you take nutrients with me?*" he asked. He levered himself down on his forelegs, placing his head at equal height with Victoria. Interlocking protective carapace slid back, revealing the slick, moist sensory band above his mandibles. The one organ took in her light, heat, and audial information.

"I'd rather eat puke, you xeno fuck," she replied. "Why do you want to eat with me anyway? If those Salvesei with the particle lancers weren't watching you'd run me down and stick me with that great big sting of yours, and I'd enjoy emptying seven rounds into your ugly face while I died."

"*It is rare to see a human outside their ship, exposed to the light instead of hiding between stars. Such a thing is to be relished, savored, tasted. You are a blight of scavengers and your breath reeks of oxygen, but you are worthy prey. I look forward to the hunt. I will see you soon, Human Victoria.*"

The Grayling lumbered away buzzing vestigial wings beneath armored plates, the Grayling equivalent of laughter.

Victoria's skin crawled. She looked over her shoulder to her escorts, "He thinks *we're* the fucking cockroaches. How do you like that?"

"Starting trouble again, are we?"

Victoria turned again at the moist warbling voice, relieved. "Hibbevox, how is Taru treating you?

"Human Victoria. I am getting too old for this excrement, if you will pardon my crassness. I wish I could have warned you of Grayling Bargult's presence aboard Taru Station. Come, perhaps you would prefer to nutrient yourself with me instead."

Hibbevox began to slide away on a slick pseudopod, sensory probes testing the air. In full height he drew himself almost up to Victoria's waist. The top of his jelly-like crown wafted in the subtle ventilation.

Victoria activated her transceiver while they followed, "Red, bad news."

"Graylings, I know, we just caught sight of one. Tohgrun?"

"Nah. If he were here I'd cast off and take my chances with running empty. I still have nightmares about his cutters. It's Bargult. But he won't wait for us to meet him in space. He'll split up, come at us inside and out." Victoria scrolled through the roster of marines in the bay until she found what she was looking for. "Baum and Webb need to go for a walk."

"I know what you have in mind. They were overdue for shore leave anyway. But that will leave bay security light."

"Have to chance it, make it happen. Where are we on the stores?"

Information streamed onto Victoria's ocular implants. She scanned through. Foodstuffs were no problem, but there was a hold on the exotic matter catalyst for the Alcubierre and the horizon drive until they could get some credit extended. Red's voice accompanied the read-out, "They're letting us load up the wagon but we need the green light. I don't think they want us here when the Gray-lings decide to make their move."

"Working on it. Sergeant, how about you?"

"Wagon's already on its way home, Captain. A Grayling on Taru? We worried?"

"Shit yes, get your ass back to the *Condor* as soon as you finish up. Double time."

They reached the pillar Hibbevox rented to manage his trade company and followed him inside, trying to ignore the pungent odor the Jenursa tended to leave where they lingered.

"Hibbe, we don't have time for lunch anymore, we re-ally need that credit unlocked."

"Regrettable, though not surprising," said Hibbevox, sliding around his desk and climbing onto a moistened reclining couch. One of his tentacles draped forward into a bowl of cultivated algae, slowly absorbing it. "You know how this works, Victoria. I cannot extend you credit unless you show me something for which the UE will reimburse my company. You have been having bad luck lately. Give me something that I might see you safely from here."

"We hit a Terygalt hulk, pulled some parts off of it."

"Yawn, Victoria. The Terygalt have little of interest to the Union Earth. Unless they have recently changed their position.

"We have live rescues."

"Compelling, but again, for the amount of exotic mat-ter you have requested? Union Earth won't pay me for your live rescues, you'll have to negotiate with their host govern-ments, and I can't ask my home office to take a loss on your

. . . unorthodox diplomacy. I need something tangible."

Victoria scowled, "Bastard, you've extended us credit for less before. You're fishing." Hibbevox's hue shifted slightly, a sign of suppressed excitement according to her ocular implants.

"Perhaps. Am I validated, human Victoria?"

Still scowling she glanced back to make sure the door was closed before reaching into her pocket and placing a piece of Malagath scrap on the table. Hibbevox leaned forward, quivering.

"Dead stars, it's true. News preceded you to Taru via our mutual friend, but I could not believe it for myself. This is their latest generation"

"And we pulled working parts out of their engine room before the Dirregaunt hit them. You know how badly Union Earth wants to get a hold of these, even hull fragments would cover our credit."

Hibbevox slid a tentacle to his radio and punched in a tonal sequence, releasing her goods for credit. Victoria's retinal implants showed the status of the auto wagons switch from *loaded* to *in transit*.

"The Jenursa will benefit greatly from this as well, human Victoria. I wish you the best speed in returning these to the Union Earth. Although, if I could persuade you to let me transport them to your government for you at no charge . . ."

"Not a chance Hibbe," she said, standing, "Even if we had time to unload it, UE would crucify me for handing over the tech to anyone. Even the Jenursa. We'll drop it ourselves, right after we take care of a few passengers."

"Your passengers take precedence? Why would Terygalt refugees take priority over functioning Malagath technology? Unless your survivors are not Terygalt . . ." he paused.

"*Dead stars,*" he hissed, "There are living Malagath aboard the *Condor*? And you *brought them to Taru*?"

Victoria winked at him.

"Madwoman, you may as well set a fire in your own ship. Tell no one of this. Go. Luck and the speed to you, Human Victoria. I pray I see you on the lee of this storm."

"A pleasure as always, Hibbe."

She turned to leave as Hibbevox received a prompt on his radio.

"Hold, Victoria. I am told one of the Grayling ships is preparing to launch."

"Can you tell me which bay?"

"I should not. But . . . 192. Use it as you will."

"Thanks Hibbe. I've got one more thing to do before I piss off. Are the FTL comm terminals on the island still secure?"

Red Calhoun relayed the information to his marines. Somewhere ahead the auto wagon sped toward the *Condor* with basic supplies and some foodstuffs for Malagath physiology. The Graylings wouldn't touch it, they wanted the warm profile of humans. But they were waiting, somewhere along the way. This was an old dance and the halls of Taru station were pocked and pitted with scorch marks, plasma stains, and more recently, bullet casings. Seven marines with him, four with Aesop and two with the captain. Eleven guarding the bay where Huian was keeping the engines warm and two more indisposed. How many Graylings were on the station? Fifty? A hundred? There was no way to know. The Vultures didn't stand a chance, separated as they were. First order, they had to link up.

On his implants, Aesop's marker closer to the *Condor*

changed from blue to red, engaged in combat. He swore, pulling up Aesop Cohen's rifle camera. Bright muzzle flashes illuminated a charging Grayling hulk, brought down before it could smash into the squad of marines. Quick bursts deterred others from remaining in line of sight as the marines retreated down an unfinished side tunnel.

"Red, contact. Graylings headed for the bay." The sergeant called in his ear, supplemented by the harsh bark of automatic rifle fire and the messy shrill of the Grayling small arms scorching the walls of the tunnels.

"God dammit, how did they find out where we moored? Never mind, can you get to us?"

Pause. More rifle fire.

"Yeah I think so; they're not pressing us but a few are shadowing."

"Keep moving lad. They're trying to surround you. We're on our way. Head to the level below you, we'll meet you at the far end of the tunnel."

His marines moved toward the markers on their implants, checking every corner and cross tunnel for Graylings. Taru station was a labyrinthine honeycomb of ancient tunnels, both natural and dug by xenos before humans ever landed on their moon.

Red spun at the skittering behind him. A single Grayling was turning the corner, long legs scrabbling for purchase. He lifted the rifle to his shoulder and squeezed a burst before Bargult could bring up his own weapon. A few of the Teflon-coated tungsten rounds ricocheted off the Grayling's protective carapace but enough penetrated, shredding the sensory band and nervous system beneath. The air filled with the smell of gunpowder. The Grayling's momentum carried it to crash into the tunnel wall as Bargult's consciousness fled it.

Red lowered his rifle and motioned to his squad. "Come on. We're made, boys," he said. He activated his transceiver, "Skipper, you finished sending your message? Things are getting hot. Can you make it to us?"

"I'm closer to Cohen, I'm going to link up with him and wait for you. No Graylings yet. I'm keeping an eye through both your implants. Try not to move your heads too much, I'm not used to seeing triple while sober."

"Aye Skipper."

The indicators for his docking bay marines went from blue to yellow.

"Report!" he shouted.

"Major, they tried to come in with the wagon, sneaky bastards. We got the door closed but it won't hold them. There's too many, and we're already light two. Looked like almost fifty of the buggers."

"Right, hold them off best you can. If you have to, retreat to the *Condor*."

"What about you?"

He frowned. "I'll figure something out. Just take as much of the bugger down as you can before you give yer ground. Don't let him bug-zap you."

Gunfire rattled in his earpiece, echoing through the tunnel shortly after. They were getting closer. He raised his gun at movement to the left. A small group of Stodun retreating from the conflict as fast as their four legs could carry them. They screamed when they saw him, but did not draw their own weapons. He spat on the tunnel floor and moved on. No one on Taru wanted to take a side between Graylings and humans, all it offered was a quick trip to the lower level kitchens.

One of his marines shouted and opened up with his rifle. Another Grayling had crashed into view while Red was distracted, knocking the marine over and putting both forelegs through his chest, piercing the composite armor like paper. Red shot it dead. Two more rounded the corner as fast as lightning and were put down by the thundering rifles. Red turned around again as the Stodun let out a second high pitched peel, warning him of another Grayling behind him. His snapshot tore apart the legs on the Grayling's left side and it collapsed, electro-plasmic discharger carving the wall beside Red with arcs of blue-white lightning. He dove to the floor behind a stalagmite and the EPD petered off as Bargult abandoned the crippled Grayling's mind to focus elsewhere.

This wasn't going well. Bargult could afford losses, Red couldn't. They couldn't fight Graylings on two fronts with six men. Something had to be done. He got to his feet and grabbed the dead marine's rifle, wedging it between the stalagmites he dodged behind. Through his suit's computer he ordered it to fire semi-randomly, and slaved its camera to his retinal implants. For good measure he left a grenade with it.

"Let's move, eyes forward," he ordered. Now with the rifle deterring pursuit, the marines fanned out in a wedge, trotting forward. Bargult prodded again, but meeting a unified front lost him three bodies before the bug could get close enough to use his weapon.

"Cohen, we're coming up on you, check your fire."

"A-firm, Major. Be advised, they're coming from a tunnel on your left. I couldn't mine it in time."

"Roger, you got eyes on the Skipper?" asked Red as he motioned for one of his marines to set an explosive. "Vick, where are you?"

The sound of a .45 automatic filled his radio. The skipper spoke after the last shots ceased. "I'm two levels up, looking at a service ladder that leads to the upper deck of the hangar. We don't have the rounds to handle more Graylings, but you better tap into the *Condor* before you worry about me.

Ahead, his squad linked up with Cohen. His marines were battered and scuffed, but none the worse for wear. Booming reports vibrated the cavern tunnels and dust shook from the sparse lighting fixtures.

"Those'd be the proximity grenades," said Cohen. Red took a look at the rifle he'd left behind. It had run empty, and Graylings were advancing up that corridor. He blew that grenade too. Then he did as the captain suggested and tapped into forward cameras on the *Condor*. The bay was swarming with Graylings.

"Huian," he said, switching to a wider channel, "You got a count on those buggers?"

"Major, this is Huian, the marines are back on board and we're sealed up tight. Bargult can't get in, but there are forty strong in the bay. Should I heat up the anti-personnel cannons?"

"Negative Miss Wong, we fire shipboard weapons in the bay and we'll never dock at Taru again. Hold fast."

"Aye Major."

He returned to the captain's channel. "Vick, they've got the bay locked down."

"I heard, asshole. Tell me something I don't know."

Bitch. He grinned. He could see her in his mind, there would be no fear in the captain's eyes, only rage and righteous indignation. He cycled through the other external cameras on the *Condor*. "They left the catwalk entrance unmanned," he said.

"That still puts us in a hangar with forty fucking Graylings," said Victoria. He could hear her eject the magazine as she spoke, checking the remaining rounds in her side-arm. Completely unnecessary as the 1911 was networked to her implants, and therefore, to his. He knew as well as she did that there were two rounds in the magazine and one in the chamber. But Victoria never trusted anything she couldn't see with her eyes. He also knew the vast majority of her spent rounds were probably lodged in some Taru bulkhead. Vick couldn't shoot for shit, and he never had figured out why every spacefaring captain seemed to gravitate to the 1911. Seven rounds weren't enough for her to hit anything.

"Don't worry, I have an idea. Stay put, Skipper," said Red. He motioned to Aesop, "Take the men, I'm transferring them under your hierarchy now. Make like you're going for the bay doors, but don't get so aggressive that he puts you down." He gestured to another of his marines, Edwards. "You, with me. We're going after the Skipper."

His marines followed Aesop, fanning out ahead to present a concave array to any Graylings. Splitting up was risky, but he needed Bargult completely focused on the bodies in the bay, so someone had to shoot at them. He and Edwards veered off into a side passage too narrow for the Graylings to follow, leading up to the next level of the station. Through Aesop's camera, he could see the exchange of fire as he engaged Bargult again. He could also see the dwindling ammo counts. *Damn,* he thought, *should have given them my spares.*

He ascended a ladder, lifting the hatch to peek through as Edwards kept an eye behind. A single Grayling patrolled the corridor. He lowered the hatch, looking to the marine just below him.

"What've we got, Major?" she whispered.

"Just one, but that's all he needs to figure out what we're

about," he replied. He radioed Aesop again, "Cohen, we need you to make him focus harder, step up your fire."

Aesop locked another magazine into his rifle. Focus harder? The Graylings were already practically turning their asses black with scorch marks from their bug-zappers. How much more focused could they get? He risked a look around the corner of the iron box that he had taken shelter behind. With no oxygen in the atmosphere there had been nothing to rust it. Funny the things you thought about when there were three meter bugs trying to fry you. Luckily the EPDs were, while destructive and deadly, relatively imprecise. Inter-Grayling warfare involved stunning rather than killing, that way you could assimilate surviving bodies. The voltage would kill a human though. If they were lucky.

He noticed something before the lash of white arcs sent him back behind the box. Only about a dozen of the Graylings were actively engaging them. Others were in the bay, either milling about or trying to crack open the *Condor*. Where was Bargult's attention if not the bay? That was obvious. *Looking for the captain.* Bargult knew she wasn't on the *Condor* yet.

"Alright, this is going to sound weird guys, but start taking shots at the ones not shooting back."

"You serious, Cohen? We're surrounded and you want us to potshot the ones that aren't already trying to cook us?"

Vega. Bit of an ass, and not just because Brazil had cleaned out the Israeli Olympic football team. "Yep," said Aesop, "And I want you to do a little samba to get their bug blood pumping for us."

"Fuck you," said Vega as he started lining up shots on

the passive Graylings.

Aesop angled his gun out from behind cover, using the camera to send a round into the back of an inactive Grayling. It squealed, and stumbled towards the bay doors, adding its EPD to the mix. Well, he supposed that could be considered a success. The other marines followed his example. Not so easy controlling a half-dozen ships, and a handful of fighters in the station, was it? More and more of the Graylings became active and brought weapons to bear.

Down to his last two magazines, Aesop hoped the captain and the major knew what they were doing.

"There, it's stopped patrolling. Let's go."

Red lifted the hatch again, carefully settling it on the deck, lest the noise alert the Grayling. It had stopped walking, or skittering or whatnot, and now stood still but for its breathing and twitching. Edwards followed closely behind as he maneuvered around the hulking xeno. He fingered a text message to Aesop on his implant's virtual keyboard, afraid the xeno might hear if he used voice comms. *Whatever it is you're doing, it's working.* He still wasn't sure it wouldn't smell them, if Graylings smelled at all.

"Can't keep it up for long, Major," came the response in his ear, "we're about dry on ammo down here."

Red kept his rifle trained on the inactive Grayling as Edwards went to the door console and released the magnetic seals for the service hatch airlock. It was too small for Graylings, so he must have left one here to make sure Victoria didn't double back. The marine muscled the door open enough to slip through, motioning him to follow. He left the Grayling and slid through the gap, pushing the door closed behind him. As Edwards shouldered open the inner door the shrill screech of the electro-plasmic weapons became almost overpowering.

Victoria stood against the wall, looking through the window in the catwalk door. He pushed past the two marines escorting her, stopping to examine a bad burn one of them had taken. When he reached her, he looked past her at the bay where most of the Graylings were saturating the open bay doors with arcs of blue-white plasmic lightning.

Together, they slid the heavy door open enough to slip through. Red crouch-walked as quietly as a man could in hard-shelled boots on metal grating, but none of the Grayling spotters had noticed them slink onto the catwalk. Bargult always held a few back with their sensory bands exposed, the rest he kept protected by the hardened interlocking plates of carapace. Almost like how the privateer marines were trained to shoot by gun cameras. Every Grayling in the bay was focused on Aesop and his marines. Red stalked to the Taru computer console above the *Condor*. It was disabled, locked for all but the Taru overseers. That wasn't much of a deterrent to the Vultures.

The staggering mental facilities of advanced spacefaring xenos was a double edged sword when it came to computers. Most were capable of mentally performing the long-form calculations required for interstellar jumps and tactical navigation unaided. Human brains simply couldn't compete, and needed computers to parse and store the data for them. The reliance on computer science had driven the advancement of processors, AI logic, network integration, and digital resolution to a level that even at first contact, was light years ahead of the neighborhood. The Union Earth didn't brag about this oversight, and so the Vultures were able to enjoy digital superiority.

The Salvesei had three main computer languages, and

the Union Earth Government cracked them decades ago. They'd changed little in the interim time, being used mainly to open doors, control lighting, and manage the artificial gravity. Two of those functions Red was particularly interested in. Following the prompts from his ocular implants Red quickly gained root access to the console, setting a few choice commands and executing a countdown script. He sent another quick message to Aesop before attaching his personal tether to the rail of the catwalk with a magnetic carabiner.

Victoria was paying more attention to the fight below when he grabbed her around the waist. She yelped in surprise, then looked at his arm around her.

"What, you want a goodbye kiss?"

He grinned, pulling the vacuum hood over his head.

"Exhale, Vick."

Her eyes went wide, "You gotta be shitting me."

Aesop was dropping his empty rifle to the sling and pulling his sidearm from the magnetic holster when he got the command to prep for vacuum and Low Gravity. That meant . . .

"*Harah*," he swore, pulling on his hood, "Hold onto something!"

The marines began to clip into whatever was handy, including other marines. Aesop made a loop from his tether and tied it under a rail. None too soon, it turned out, as the major's hack kicked in. First, the local gravity dissipated as the artificial gravity generators for the bay were shut off. The asteroid barely had enough mass to keep them floating off, and the Graylings noticed the change. Aesop felt himself sliding back against the metal crate as the natural vector took over. The hail of plasma cut off abruptly as the Graylings scrabbled for purchase inside the bay and began sliding towards the rear of the hangar. Then the exterior airlock opened, evacuating the entire bay to space. Something as massive as the *Condor* didn't move much, but the rushing nitrogen atmosphere raced to meet the vacuum, carrying the Graylings with it. Aesop and the marines were pulled taught against their tethers. A massive form tumbled past him, shattering a stalactite and continuing on to the bay airlock.

Sirens sounded in the station as every connecting airlock in the vicinity slammed shut, but were silenced as the last of the air fled. The furious rushing pull on Aesop and the other marines lessened as the vacuum normalized and gravity returned. Warning lights still flashed, but the sirens were now a hollow vibration translating through the walls and the soles of his boots. Sparse fire returned from behind where a few remaining Graylings had found something to cling to, but the bay ahead was empty. Gravity returned, the entire episode had lasted maybe a few seconds.

"Move, marines!" he shouted. He stood, emptying the magazine in his sidearm at Bargult's remaining Graylings as he dashed to the bay. The Graylings couldn't pursue; they could last longer than humans in a vacuum but it was still lethal to them within minutes.

Captain Victoria had a vague sensation of dropping as Red lowered them with the tether. She hit the ground and almost collapsed. Her lungs were on fire. She was on fire all over, why was she so hot? Shouldn't she be freezing? Even her tongue felt bubbly, but it was hard to tell with all the black crowding the edges of her vision. Her footsteps sounded odd, and she saw other dark shapes around her, and ahead, was that the *Condor?* Jesus why did everything hurt so bad, was she dead? Her ears felt like they'd exploded, her sinuses like something had crawled inside, and her eyes like they didn't fit in her head. Warnings flashed on one of her retinal implants, but she couldn't read them. Everything was blurry.

She saw a hand as she was shoved to the floor of the *Condor's* airlock. Her hand. It was all blue under the nails, that wasn't right. That . . . wasn't . . . right.

A hiss, and suddenly she could inhale. She gasped, face against the metal deck of the *Condor's* cargo bay. She was burning hot, but no sweat covered her. It had boiled off in the vacuum. If it was possible she hurt even more now, in her head, in every joint. She remembered . . . remembered . . .

Decompression

Hypoxia

Vacuum

"Bargult," she stammered.

Her marine major leaned down beside her, "Take it easy, Vick, we've got it from here."

"Bullshit, control, now. That's a direct fucking order, Major," she said. She was lucky to even be conscious. Red must have gotten her from the catwalk to the aft airlock in just a couple seconds, her legs working on autopilot. They didn't seem to want to work now, that was for damn sure.

Red looked unhappy, she almost never used his title, never pulled rank on him. But he looped her arm around his shoulder and helped her up two decks to the conn, passing awed marines and crew. The First Prince was there, face placid and emotionless. How much had he seen?

Huian already maneuvered the ship out of the bay door when Victoria slid into her captain's chair. The view screen was bright with the Graylings Red had shoved into space. They were out there, dying. Not fast enough for her. She wiped blood from underneath her nose. Burst capillaries most likely, but she was returning to herself. Her cyanosis was fading, too.

"Captain Marin has the deck and the conn. Carillo, light those fuckers up."

Now outside the Taru Station hangar, the prohibition of shipboard weapons was lifted. The first prince hissed audibly as the ship's two forward point-defense cannons individually targeted and shredded every free-floating Grayling in less than the span of a breath with a storm of metal shards. The smaller hostile carrots on the tactical screen fell away, replaced by a single contact. The Grayling ship accelerating on the other side of the station.

"Huian, ahead three-point-five, roll us belly out and take us along towards the planet."

"Three-point-five aye, ma'am."

"Steady as she bears. Avery, what have you got?"

"He's lit up Skipper, active sweep on multiple frequencies, over the horizon of Taru but we're getting their bounce off the local moon. Attenuator?"

"Negative, I want him to see us. Increase speed and flash our pipes, just enough to let him feel clever. Make him work for it."

"Aye Skipper"

The *Condor* accelerated past the horizon of Taru Station, the jagged red silhouette of the Grayling cutter emerging against the local star. Warning klaxons sounded as the privateer ship was directly exposed to Bargult's active sensors, showing her entire dorsal profile. He immediately began to accelerate towards the *Condor*.

"Con sensors, his weapons are heating up."

"Huian, cut acceleration, pull him away from Taru. Tactical, deploy electric chaff."

"Con tactics aye," said her XO from the fire control center.

A small missile separated from the *Condor*, intercepting the blue-white fire that lanced out from the Grayling cutter. It burst in a hail of conductive material, creating a screen that matched the momentum of the *Condor*. The Grayling weapon, fired from only a few kilometers away, began to chew through the screen at an alarming rate.

"Skipper he's maneuvering."

"I see him. Huian, keep the screen between us. We need him further from Taru."

"Aye ma'am."

The First Prince examined the tactical display, "This creature, this . . . Bargult, he is using the station to prevent you firing upon him?"

"Captain he's cutting through the screen, it'll only last a few more seconds."

"Aye, Prince, but it won't help him. He was dead the second he decided to chase the *Condor*. Carillo, that's all we need. Blow it on my mark, steady, steady . . . mark!"

The plasmic lightning halted as fire erupted out of the Grayling ship. It spun, rocked by the explosion and venting the hellish atmosphere within the ship. Radiation levels spiked on the sensors enough to trigger a proximity alert, the core of the cutter had compromised and begun venting a wake of burning blue vapor. What was left of the hulk continued on a ballistic course towards the open arms of the uninhabited first planet.

"How . . . ? Captain Marin?" murmured the First Prince.

Victoria winked at him, trying to ignore the searing pain in her eye as she did. She also noticed why her retinal implants were so damn blurry, one of them had cracked in the vacuum. "Space walkers," was the only reply she offered.

"Helm, bear for a swing around the planet. Let's get the First Prince and his crew home before Bargult decides he needs more of a beating."

On the black rocky surface of Taru Station, Tessa Baum and her partner-in-crime Aimes Webb watched the light of the *Condor* disappear over the horizon of the planet. The Grayling cutter they tagged with a handheld exotic-matter bomb as it emerged from hangar 192 burned brilliantly between the station and the dark side of the planet. Two other Grayling ships were launching but the *Condor* was long gone, having used the planet's gravity to slingshot themselves toward the local star for a horizon jump. Bargult made no move to retrieve the burning derelict. The same ruptured plasmic core that made for such a bright display made it too dangerous to approach. It didn't matter, Bargult would make another. Grayling ships were formed from a natural resin derived from the trees they cultivated on their home planet. Go figure, the only xenos sailing around the stars in wooden ships.

Before they had lost contact with the *Condor's* computers they knew that the dead Grayling ship would continue to burn along its present course until it sheared itself apart in the planet's atmosphere in several hours.

"So what now? There are still Graylings on the station," Aimes asked over his radio.

Tessa looked at her fellow marine, completely matte black in his vacuum suit and hard-shell helmet. The black silhouette of a man with a rifle. *Nothing rattles, nothing shines,* was what her grandfather used to say.

"Red said to get in contact with Jenursa Hibbevox. He'll hide us until another privateer shows up that we can hitch on with. Maybe the *Sagan* or the *Huxley*."

"So I suppose we're done with the Vulture?"

"For now, babe, we're on vacation. And I can only think of about a half-dozen people I'd rather spend it with."

"Yeah but how many of them love you like I do?"

"None," she said, playfully pushing him. He lost his balance in the miniscule gravity offered by the station beyond the generators, tumbling briefly until he could latch his magnetic boots onto an iron plate. He laughed over the radio.

"Hey Tessa, how's your O2 culture?" he asked.

"Good, why?"

"Well," Aimes gestured to the disabled cutter, "That's got to be the biggest confirmed kill of our privateer careers, why not stay out a while and milk it? Hibbevox isn't going anywhere and the Graylings are probably still riled up."

Tessa snorted, "Oh yeah, a vacuum suit climbing up my colon and a burning Grayling cutter. The pinnacle of romance," she said. Despite her tone she slowly walked to Aimes and sat down next to him. "It is kind of pretty in a morbid sort of way."

Silence passed between the two marines for a time before the local sun grew dark.

"Nighttime on Taru already?" asked Tessa. She felt a tug on his shoulder, pulling her to her feet.

"Tess, we need to get to Hibbevox. Right now."

"What about the Graylings?"

"Fuck the Graylings. Look."

Tessa followed the pointing finger of Aimes to the false sunset created by the massive ship blocking the light of the star. Where before had been empty space, now floated the *Springdawn*.

CHAPTER 5
THE LESSER EMPIRES

BEYOND THE ASTEROID station, an alien ship burned. Best Wishes didn't know her name or what race had crewed her as she plummeted towards the shadow of the planet. There was no archival data on this system, or the independent space station that had surely been the destination of their mystery vessel. Was that his unknown quarry burning up in the atmosphere? It was still uncertain, as was their relationship with the *Dreadstar* before his arrival. They had been drawn by the distress call, most likely. Picked the bones of the dead ship and hastened away before his science team could extrapolate the interstellar coordinates. But one had to be certain. Best Wishes' claws clicked on his bone spurs as he considered. He was tempted to put the lesser empire ship out of its misery, the scans had indicated levels of radiation lethal to nearly all known species.

His first officer, Modest Bearing, approached as he watched the ship begin to burn up in the atmosphere.

"Commander, we are in contact with the administrator of the colony. He calls himself a Salvesei, and evidently we are in their empire, though he makes no claim that we violated their sovereign territory. He was very particular about this. I believe he wanted to ensure that we were not offended. He informed us that this is a neutral station, and asks how we might be served."

Fear bred humility, as was proper from the lesser empires. No one would dare suggest that the Dirregaunt should not go where they pleased. Best Wishes would show respect and amnesty to those who knew their place.

"Tell the Taru administrator that we require a bay for our shuttles and to make ready to receive the commander of the *Springdawn*. No ships are to leave the station save ours. Any violators of this condition will be fired upon and we will not look kindly toward the station should they facilitate this."

"Commander, you intend to go aboard yourself? This lesser empire outpost is dangerous, filled with delinquents and savages. It's not safe, let me go in your stead."

Best Wishes laid his ears flat in respect to his friend and first officer, "No, you will have the *Springdawn* until my return. This is something I must do myself. I am lacking . . . perspective, shall we say. I have hunted the Malagath Empire and Kossovoldt for all my life but I am ignorant in the ways of our new quarry. To hunt something you must know its ways. I would learn of them firsthand."

"As you say, Commander. In that case, with your permission, I would like to rotate men on and off the station so as many as possible might learn what hides in uncivilized space. Also, I shall accompany you, Measured Calm can watch the ship as well as I. My duties aboard the *Coalescence* included many instances of contact with the savage regions of the void and its inhabitants, I will go so that you have someone with firsthand experience."

And so that he would have someone to watch his back, he suspected. "And what does your experience tell you of this place?"

Modest Bearing gestured to the screen as the unknown ship began to break apart, trailing smoke and plasma down through the planet's atmosphere where it ignited pockets of hydrogen.

"Ask them, Commander."

———

"You should be just fine, Skipper. Aside from the swelling, burst capillaries, and aftereffects of decompression sickness, a minor case of the bends is the worst I'm seeing. But I wouldn't go doing that again without a suit. And that right retinal implant is going to need to come out next shore leave."

"Thanks Doc, I agree. It was a shitty plan," said Victoria. She had refused to leave the captain's chair in the conn of the *Condor* despite the relative safety of the horizon jump so Red had ordered the ship's medic up to check her out. Everyone on board had triage training, but only Doc Whipple had a medical license and battlefield surgery experience. He had been a colonel in the Air Force, a field surgeon before signing on to patch up the privateers. The Vultures kept him busy.

"Worked though," said Red.

"Doesn't make it any less shitty. You're sure my eyes aren't about to fall out, Doc?"

"Quite sure, Vick."

"Feels like it. Christ," she said, pulling her overshirt back on.

"Oh and no alcohol for two weeks"

"What'll happen if I drink alcohol, Doc?"

"Probably nothing, but you drink too much."

"Get the fuck off my conn."

"Suit yourself, Vick," said the Doc. He repacked his

kit and made his way from the conn, nodding to the First Prince on his way through the door. Tavram nodded back before striding forward in the limited space offered him. The conn had become his typical haunt, given that he spent significant time on starship bridges. The other members of the Malagath Empire had taken to exploring the ship and some were even assisting in the early stages of repair.

"He is not incorrect, Captain Marin. Many a great military mind has been reduced by overconsumption of intoxicants," he said. "During the great expansion we warred with a militant empire, the Vvanay. They were ruthless and efficient, conquerors and scorchers of worlds. Not a terrible threat to us, you understand, but with skill and territory enough to stymie our march toward the core for the time being."

He relaxed onto the first officer's chair, though almost comically large for it, if anything about the severe alien could be said to be comical. XO Carillo rarely frequented the conn, preferring to carry out his administrative duties in the fire control station where he directed the tactical weapons team.

"So what happened to them?" asked Victoria.

"We began to notice a decrease in their ability to wage war in space. Their fleet maneuvers became sluggish, their targeting solutions sloppy. Navigators miscalculated space tears and vessels were lost in the space between stars. Even their logistics network began failing to make appropriate deliveries, which we discovered when several of our ambushes failed to produce a single cargo ship. We believed it to be war fatigue, but our intelligence discovered an intoxicant spreading through their military ranks. While pleasurable, the drug bore long-term negative effects on cognition. They acquired it from one of the lesser empire planets they conquered, the name of which was likely never recorded. The addiction spread through their population like a disease and decimated their ability to calculate interstellar jumps. It crippled their entire empire."

"And then you moved in for an easy kill."

Tavram made a strange gesture that Victoria's remaining retinal implant told her meant an aggressive affirmative. "We cut into them from the outside, and encountered the Kossovoldt coming from the galactic core. Then the true war began. The day we clashed with the Kossovoldt in the center of the Vvanay territory, we learned what a real enemy looked like."

Victoria shivered, to be caught between the Malagath and the Kossovoldt . . . damn. She tried to imagine the two species blasting each other over the red-scorched skies of Earth while humanity watched helplessly from below.

Tavram continued, "Of course we learned much later that the Kossovoldt had engineered the intoxicant which led to the total downfall of the Vvanay and seeded it on worlds that fit the colonization criterion. Had they not, your people might have called us the Big Four, instead of the Big Three. Now the Vvanay are a broken people, clinging to a dozen worlds, all too insignificant for us to bother stamping out. They continue to survive because the Malagath and Kossovoldt are waiting for the other to expend the resources to finish the genocide we started 5000 years ago. This is why Malagath Imperials are forbidden from intoxicants while serving my father's armada, and in the militaries of our vassal empires."

"I suppose it's a good thing I'm not military, then."

"No? And yet you engineered the destruction of a hostile ship before they had even left the station without even heating up your primary weapons. Even more impressive if you are civilians. I sympathize with the lesser empire that must someday face your military."

"They don't need your sympathy, Prince Tavram. The privateers have the best ships humanity can field, and it's the bare minimum we need to survive. The few times our military clashed with someone else we found ourselves on the wrong end of an interstellar ass-whipping. That's how the privateers came about," said Victoria. She rubbed her eyes, still sore from the brief exposure to the vacuum. She wasn't looking forward to the surgery required to fix the broken implant, it required the subject to remain conscious.

"Perhaps they do not, but it is not your technology that impresses, Captain. What was the term your friend Red used previously, 'Meanest sons of bitches in space?'"

Victoria grinned, "I take it you were watching us give those bug-faced bastards hell?"

"Indeed, your administrative officer allowed me access to the cameras on the weapons of several of your . . . marines? Is the nomenclature? Curious that you name your planet dirt and your warriors water. But your men—"

"And women," Victoria interjected pointedly.

". . . And women, Captain, handle those weapons as if born to them. To the Malagath, infantry tactics are an antiquity, a relic left behind."

"Believe me, First Prince. Humanity has been trying to leave it behind for millennia. We just can't seem to shake the habit."

"If you are any indication, I would postulate that humans are a quarrelsome and unlikable people."

Victoria coughed, startled. "Unlikable?"

"Perhaps. I am grown fond of your crew, but I must admit that from the outside I initially saw you as brash, abrasive, uncivilized, possessed of a superiority complex, and prone to attracting conflict on account of your egos. Capable? Obviously. Competent? Without question. But insolent, and hard to tolerate. Tell me, why do the Grah'lhin so despise humans?"

"Because they damn well first saw us as prey. Weak, hiding in the shadows like cowards unwilling to stand up and fight. Then we bit back, showed that this cat has claws. Then instead of moving in for the kill we retreated, inviting them to try again at their peril. They can't reconcile that dichotomy of being dangerous but not a danger. Of being weaker but not stamped out."

The first prince stroked his neck glands in thought, "And how many of the other lesser empires have so reconciled? How many would prey on you if they knew where your empire lay?"

Victoria counted in her head, "Including the Graylings, a half dozen? Maybe as many as nine? The only planets we let the rest of the galaxy see are cohabitates though, they would have to declare war on the Jenursa or Thorivult to attack those. All of the full-human colonies are kept very hidden."

"Let us say seven empires. How long ago was your first contact?"

"Almost 200 years ago, Kosso Standard, but we had known we weren't alone for almost 40 years prior."

"Two hundred years, with no military presence so to speak, and already seven empires have desire to war with you. Most of which likely can't live on your oxygen-rich planets. By the time you have been in space as long as the Malagath Empire you will be at war with everyone in the galaxy. To use nautical terminology of which you are so fond, you are a small boat in a large ocean, making noticeable waves."

"Hell, the Orion Spur is barely even aware we exist. We're not even in the damn databases of most xenos."

"And how do you know this?"

Victoria was silent. She couldn't tell him that humanity had broken into the woefully pitiful computer systems of almost every race still using some sort of programming language to code their ship networks. Computers were the one area where humanity was ahead of the competition. Couldn't tell him that Earth was sifting through billions of pages of historical data from across their local neighborhood, including history on the Malagath Empire. Knowledge was one of the few powers humans had in this new, unfriendly sea of stars.

"Alas, Captain Marin, I am given to understand that it will be some time before we reach the next station. I shall retire to see to the needs of my crew. Captain Marin, Human Huian."

The First Prince stood, bowing out of the conn through the hatch. Victoria crossed her legs over the arms of the captain's couch, relaxing as much as she could.

"Huian, he hangs around here so much I might as well make him the captain. What's your read of him?"

"I don't think I'm qualified to say, ma'am."

Victoria scowled, "Leave the fucking blue-water politicking back on Earth where it belongs, Huian. I hate that shit, and just having you here reminds me how much. Don't gripe about putting a foot wrong and mucking up your next review. That's not how it works up here. Answer the question."

Victoria's helmsman shrank under the withering barrage. She knew it was unfairly cruel, and Huian was proving herself a capable pilot, against all odds. But she would always be the UE's eyes and ears aboard the *Condor.* Her family had jumped her to the head of the line over other, more qualified pilots, and Victoria was worried she had brought bad habits from the Chinese blue-water Navy with her. At least her watch station was somewhere Victoria could keep an eye on.

"I think," said Huian, choosing her words with care, "He is very severe. He is polite, but not friendly. And . . . less haughty than I would have expected for someone known across 40,000 worlds. He would make a good ally."

"Make no mistake, Huian. He is not our ally in any sense of the word. If his ship had been operational when we came across it and we weren't running the gravitic stealth until we knew his weapons were offline, he'd have atomized us like we would swat a fucking fly. I'm not convinced he still won't as soon as we turn him over. We're *lesser empire*, didn't you know? I need some sort of assurance."

"What do you have in mind, Ma'am?"

Victoria sighed, "I don't know yet," she said. She sat for a time in silence pondering it over.

"Captain," Huian began, "Were you able to send a crypto to my mother? We could see the marine rifle cameras, but yours and Red's implant cams are locked out and the XO didn't want the First Prince to know about them."

"Hmm? Oh, yes Huian. I sent the message. A response will be waiting for us at the listening post near Pilum Forel. I hope. You should familiarize yourself with that local cluster, there's a lot there."

"I already have, Ma'am."

Victoria paused, "Yeah, I suppose you would have," she said. Victoria stood, "I'll be in my stateroom, growl me if anything interesting happens."

"Goodnight, ma'am."

———

"Esteemed Commander, welcome to Taru Station."

Best Wishes climbed down from the launch, feeling the rough rocky surface of the Taru hangar bay beneath his bare feet. His four eyes scanned in different directions, except for the one focused on the station administrator. The Salvesei was a slim and bony biped, with a wide crested skull and an array of shiny black eyes beneath. It wore a uniform bereft of any rank or insignia. A civilian then? He clicked his back teeth together in annoyance. Useless bureaucrats, they wore rules and regulations like a coat and concerned themselves more with their own position than the task at hand. They squabbled and clucked over their pieces of the lesser empires, not knowing how little they mattered in the universe.

"My thanks, Salvesei . . . ?"

"Gaelif, Commander. We are eager to assist the Dirregaunt however we may."

"Gaelif, yes. We hunt a ship; it would have arrived within the past Kosso standard day. Once we find it we will depart this system."

"Gracious Commander, as you no doubt saw yourself, this station services hundreds of ships daily, from dozens of empires. Almost 75,000 are aboard Taru Station at any particular time."

Best Wishes padded forward. From a distance, he examined the armed guards Administrator Gaelif had brought with him. He could hear their heartbeats, see their flitting eyes, almost feel the heat as their hands gripped primitive particle lancers. Nervousness was universal, and it was evident upon all of them. Clearly the Salvesei had evolved from a species of prey rather than predator. He wondered if the next rung of their food chain still stalked the primal jungles of their home world.

"Yes I saw. And once we have what we seek they will be free to leave the station once more. Tell me, do you feel this armed detail necessary?"

The Taru administrator chittered under his breath, something in his native language to which Best Wishes was not privy. A curse, perhaps?

"There are likely those aboard the station who feel their business is being harmed by the delay. Who would not be as hospitable as I am," said Gaelif.

Who have lost family and friends to the Dirregaunt.

"They would attack, even with the threat of my vessel hanging over them?"

"In so many words, no. An outright attack is unlikely. But were any of your crew to wander away from the security detail I could not guarantee their safety."

"Then for the sake of their business and your station it would be prudent to waste little time. Our scan detected a major population center. Take me there, open access to your global communication circuit, and we will begin."

Best Wishes, his First Officer, and his Sensor Officer followed Gaelif out of the hangar and onto a small vehicle which hummed a few inches above the uneven floor of the tunnel. It shifted slightly as the three Dirregaunt and the Taru administrator climbed aboard. Imperfect gravitic technology. The ride would be bumpy.

"We have made several such skiffs available, Commander. I am given to understand that many of the *Springdawn's* crew have been given leave to explore the station. For your privacy we have assigned you a hangar quite distant to the primary hub."

Best Wishes ignored him as he examined the walls of the tunnel. Hardly a few meters passed in between sections scorched by small arms fire. Through his top eye he even spotted some plasma residue that still carried radiated heat. A dangerous place indeed.

Modest Bearing had engaged the administrator on the topic of the station's history and formation as the Taru had colonized it. The administrator was happy to distract himself with details of the station's construction. The hive of tunnels and caverns was completely sealed to space by hundreds of airlocks, and the microgravity controlled by countless gravitic manipulators toward the purpose of easing traversal and freight operations. The station itself, he learned, had been in operation for nearly 800 standard years through several geopolitical changes on Salvesei itself. Interstellar trade tariffs and docking fees in the station were a major source of income for the Salvesei, whose total population across all colonies and their home world amounted to a number in the low dozens of billions. Barely a blip, compared to the Dirregaunt.

Best Wishes leaned back and hung his hands on his bone protuberances as the skiff sped from the tunnels into the brilliant light of the central hub. Towering columnar buildings twisted into a cavern so high it was obscured by a dark cloud cover. Lights could be seen refracted by the fog. All of the huge buildings were natural stone formations, likely excavated to form chambers and rooms, rented out to local empires by the Salvesei.

The ground level was littered with fabricated metal buildings and packed with as many races as Best Wishes had ever seen in one place. Many of them openly stared at the skiff, curious about the Dirregaunt commander holding the station hostage. Modest Bearing renewed his barrage of questions on the administrator and Best Wishes found a moment of privacy with his sensor officer, Dutiful Heiress. Such moments had been difficult for him to arrange over the duration of the mission. He took in the sight of her studying the architecture of Taru Station.

"I would hear your thoughts, Dutiful," he whispered, so as not to attract the attention of the rest of their party.

The officer pulled her attention away from the city and focused her keen eyes on Best Wishes. It took effort to keep his heart from accelerating to a degree she might notice.

"Are there many places such as this outside the core worlds? I did not think the lesser empires capable of such construction. I can put name to perhaps one in ten of these creatures. Forty thousand worlds in the Dirregaunt Praetory and we are the outsiders here."

"We are not in the Praetory, my friend. It is easy to forget that any of the lesser empires, while scattered and primitive, might one day stand as equals. But today the affairs of the Malagath Empire and the Dirregaunt, normally so far above them, have directly interceded in their lives. Remember them well. Though you will likely never see them again they will never forget this day."

She turned back towards them. "What you say is true, my Commander."

"Dutiful," said Best Wishes, unsure of how to continue, "have you considered staying aboard the *Springdawn* once the mission is over?"

She snapped her attention back to him. "Commander, I . . . You know my duty is to my house and my caste. I was born to it, *named* for it. To ignore the purpose of my calling would bring great shame."

The skiff slid up to a polycrete platform aside a fabricated metal building crowned with a multitude of antennae and cables stretching up into the cloud bank. A light precipitation of condensate nitrogen had begun to fall in the hub, cool droplets splashing on Best Wishes' head and neck, immediately boiling off into gas. His ears twitched, attuning themselves to the change in the acoustics. He could tell where rain landed on flesh versus metal and stone. He looked up at the cloud cover in the upper cavern. Was it actually a cooling system for the massive station?

"I am not asking you to forsake your family. You are a fine officer, and another tour would see you likely captain of your own ship."

"How altruistic your offer, commander, to bear me onboard another three years to advance my career," she said flatly.

Blood drained from his face. He had been too obvious. But *there*, the corners of her eyes twisting up. She was teasing him. Perhaps there was yet the possibility.

"In truth I have considered what it might be like to command a vessel of my own. I have learned much in the sensor centers on *Springdawn*, though not as much as I have learned on the bridge. There is a peculiar energy to the way you hunt Malagath. Even now."

"You don't feel as though I'm being obsessively thorough?" asked Best Wishes.

"Perhaps, but if it leads us to places such as this," she said, gesturing around them as the skiff pulled up to a docking clutch, "then I would like to see where else it takes us."

They unloaded outside a permanent building with a bristling coat of antennae and sprawling tentacles of thick wire. Modest Bearing gave him a significant look as they disembarked. He had been listening to Best Wishes' conversation. From the tilt of his eyes it was clear he did not approve. Administrator Gaelif ushered them inside where several other Salvesei manned a variety of large consoles covered in dials, switches, lights, and plugs.

"This is the central communication switch where we route all communication through the station. From here we can access any connected speaker, amplifier, vidscreen, or luminous display, wired or otherwise. We have prepared it for your use, commander," he said. Gaelif lifted a wired microphone to his small, flat mouth.

"Attention Taru Station," he said. Outside of the communications center Best Wishes could hear the message being repeated over speakers built throughout the city. "As you are all aware, a Dirregaunt dreadnaught has temporarily barred egress from the station. The commander of this dreadnaught is here with me now to make clear the terms of his visit. I am handing the communicator to him now."

Best Wishes accepted the small blue disc, careful not to scratch the surface with his claws. He raised it to his mouth.

"Good day, Taru Station. I am the commander of the Dirregaunt vessel *Springdawn*. I track a fugitive ship of unknown origin. We determined that it rode the stars to this system approximately half a standard day ago, likely for repair and refit at this station. Once I find it and its commander I will depart Taru Station. If it has already departed, we require information about their destination. Of our quarry we know this: their propulsion system used accelerated xenon ions. All knowledge of these spacefarers delivered to the central communication switch will be rewarded. That is all."

"Whatever you two fools are planning, I must protest." said Hibbevox. Tessa and Aimes scanned through the directory of Union Earth equipment in the storeroom.

Officially it was all registered under Hibbevox's holdings aboard Taru Station, but it contained everything from replacement starship parts to munitions and vacuum suits.

"We can't pass up an opportunity like this, Hibbe. Those shuttles are live Dirregaunt tech, even just a look inside is worth more than everything in this storehouse. If we manage to *steal* something? Well, I don't have to tell you what that would mean."

Hibbevox vibrated visibly, turning a deep shade of purple, "It means they'd lance this station with enough radiation to cook you both into steak, and damned be the rest of the population. You can't just kill Dirregaunt spacefarers and not expect repercussions."

"We may not have to, Tessa look at this," said Aimes. He swiveled his panel towards her. She laughed.

"Nice find, do you think it still works?"

Hibbevox slid forward reluctantly, "What did you find?" he asked. Tessa lowered the panel so that the diminutive alien could take a look, though she was completely oblivious how the Jenursa processed sensory input, they looked like nothing so much as the lovechild of a mushroom and a jellyfish.

"It's a rifle attachment, Hibbe. A tranquilizer mod for the forward rail on the X-87's. See this tank? It's a refrigerant. Once it's introduced to the cartridges in the receiver it shoots a frozen needle of concentrated sedative from this secondary barrel, which melts as soon as it pierces skin and disperses into the body. We don't generally use them anymore. Xenos mostly come aboard willingly when we dock, not like when we first started privateering."

"And you just happen to have sedative effective with Dirregaunt biochemistry laying around? *Humans.* Why am I not surprised?" asked Hibbevox.

"No," said Aimes, "But we can synthesize it. The device to make the rounds is part of the mount's package."

"You're going to get us all killed."

"Well hey," said Tessa, "It's better than skulking around in these ridiculous hooded cloaks like a medieval vagabond waiting for some xeno to realize there are still humans aboard Taru. The last place the Dirregaunt would think to look for us is in their hangar bay."

"I suppose in your twisted little human mind that makes sense," said Hibbevox. Whatever he was about to say next was cut off as the main circuit crackled to life from the various speakers installed in the walls of the storeroom.

"*Attention Taru Station.*"

"That's Administrator Gaelif," said Hibbevox. Tessa shushed him. The three listened to the introduction, and then to barking tones of the Dirregaunt commander. Aimes groaned at the conclusion of the message.

"That's it, Tess, he's got us dead to rights. Who else uses xenon fueled ion engines?"

"Perhaps not, not every empire does a full spectrum analysis of every ship they come across, and many have never met your ship in the void. *And* not every privateer uses identical propulsion systems. It is not common knowledge," said Hibbevox, leaving a slimy trail towards the door and his waiting skiff.

"Hey Hibbe, where you going?" probed Tessa.

"Isn't it obvious? To the communication hub."

Heat flushed Tessa's cheeks, "You traitorous little gelatin cube!" she shouted. Hibbevox turned a vibrant red.

"*Think*, human Tessa. I'm the foremost authority on your species on this station. If they call upon me perhaps I can learn what they know. More importantly, I can find out what they learn from the one other entity on-station with knowledge of human presence at a Malagath wreck."

"Bargult."

"Bingo, as you humans say. He's probably on his way to the communication switch right now."

He slipped towards the door, brushing a slimy tentacle against the access pad. As the door opened he began to slide through, but stopped. Tessa wasn't sure how, but she got the impression that the Jenursa had turned toward her.

"My office is not safe for you now. My company maintains a private residence on the second shell, section 452 room 12. No one will look for you there. Please, counter to your species' insane, suicidal nature, do not do anything foolish."

The door slid closed and Tessa was left alone with Aimes. She looked at him, a half grin across her face.

"Insane? Suicidal? Foolish? Us? Who does he think we are?"

"No idea, Tess. Ooh, look! EM grenades!"

Best Wishes was growing frustrated. Thus far in the time since his broadcast, now set to repeat every twenty degrees of the local star's journey across the planet of Taru, he had received naught but fools and charlatans. Who were these imbecilic cretins believing themselves wise to waste his time? Did they not know that lies were universal? That he could smell the stink of their nervous breath upon the air, even past his supplemental breathing stream? That he could hear their hearts beat faster and see the blood heat underneath their skin as they spun their falsehoods in hopes of meager scraps from his table?

He turned to his sensor officer, "Perhaps our ship did not dock at the station after all? There is little knowledge of it."

Instead of answering, Dutiful Heiress' eyes grew wide and she bared her teeth. "Dead stars," she swore under her breath. Best Wishes found himself momentarily confused by a new scent in the air until a low hissing voice behind him uttered a single word.

"Humans."

He turned, staring down the largest primal horror of chitinous legs and oily carapace he had ever seen. Every creeping crawling skittering nasty he had seen planet side had been supersized and dressed in glossy black. Shiny mandibles large enough to crush his head hovered just before his face.

"You seek humans. Xenon ionic propulsion present at a Malagath wreck. I am correct, yes?"

Best Wish's heart attempted to beat its way out of his chest. He steeled himself, taking manual control over the organ and slowing his heart rate. *By the Praetor*, this thing even sounded like a jungle full of insects when it spoke. Physiologically speaking, a creature like this shouldn't exist, it should be collapsing under its own weight.

And yet it wasn't wrong. They mentioned nothing in the broadcast of a Malagath wreck. And the name, *humans*, had an ominous feel. A genuine feel. This was no charlatan. He could hardly believe such a creature to be a fool.

"How do you know of this?" asked Best Wishes. One eye swiveled, noting the Taru security force arraying themselves along the edge of the platform. The creature must have noticed them too, it extended onto the tips of its legs, though how it saw them was a mystery. He could see no eyes.

"We shall converse over nutrients. Come, eat, sustain," it said, and began jilting away on long legs."

Best Wishes leapt down from the platform behind the creature. The voice of Modest Bearing called out behind him.

"Commander, wait," he said.

Best Wishes turned briefly, "I have waited long enough. I grow hungry, for food and information. You wait here should you wish, and interview anyone else who comes by," he said. He eyed a small slimy alien moving towards the hub. "Look, there is your next interviewee."

He looked as though he wanted to join him, but eyeing the giant creature he backed away. He was swift and brilliant, but bravery was not favored among his qualities. Luckily, Best Wishes had use for an officer that counseled caution. Just not at the moment. The security detail made to follow him but a raised hand held them in place. One leaned down at the edge of the platform.

"Take care, Commander. They are dangerous beings."

"Who, the insects?"

"Yes. But I was referring to humans. You saw the aftermath of their anger when you arrived. If it is them you are seeking, be wary."

So the Salvesei knew of them too. Why had they said nothing? Perhaps he should have words with the administrator on his return.

He made his way after the plodding alien, obviously in no hurry despite the path that cleared before it. It walked with a strange canter, as if its attention were elsewhere. Best Wishes followed closely behind, claws resting upon his bone protuberances. It led him below the primary level of the city, into a literal underworld, a layer deeper in the rock of the station. Immediately the population became less savory. Clearly, Taru Station was not free of crime and poverty if the destitute urchins were any indication.

Families and gangs huddled in the muck that lined the tunnel walls, eying the pair but not approaching. Here the waste of the central hub gravitated, without purpose or place. He suspected that the Salvesei gave up trying to herd them together and ship them off station. There were too many places down here to run, too many to hide and the deprived knew it better than the security forces ever would. Between the gang graffiti and the smell of unwashed bodies he could see the odd handheld maser and other presumably illegal contraband changing hands. As the minutes passed he heard his own recorded broadcast, muffled through the stone and steel of the station. Whatever audio equipment may once have been here had long since been salvaged for parts.

Best Wishes' guide seemed to be heading for a cavern from which the unmistakable smell of cooked fat and meat wafted. A cantina then. He had passed several on his way to the communication switch, serving patrons with protein constructions and amino acid supplements shaped and flavored with the tastes of their own planets and tuned to their biochemistry. Where had this one gotten real meat?

Ducking into the dimly lit cantina, he was greeted with a menagerie of predatory looking aliens hunched over private tables eating, or consuming intoxicants, from the pungent smell. Some conversation quieted as they noticed the massive alien lumbering towards an area big enough to seat it comfortably. Best Wishes slid onto a chair opposite as it arrayed its many limbs in what he assumed was a comfortable position.

A section of carapace on the creature's head slid back, revealing a slick black membrane with a wet glossy sheen. A sensory band, like the Kossovoldt, though unidirectional.

"Do you know what I am, Dirregaunt hunter?" it asked.

Again, the strange low chirping behind the words, as though they were being synthesized instead of constructed with vocal chords.

"No, your empire is unfamiliar," replied Best Wishes.

"I am Grah'lhin, many from one. I too am a hunter. I am called Bargult. I sit before you, I stand upon the prow gazing at Malagath fragments many stars away, and beyond Taru Station I burn as radiation bleeds from my ship and vacuum ruptures my organs. Do you understand?"

"No," said Best Wishes. How could he? It sounded like inane babble. Could this forsaken creature really have useful information?

Bargult's mandibles clicked together appreciably, *"There are few who do, Dirregaunt hunter. I know what it is you would track. Human Victoria and her Vultures."*

Victoria. He didn't know what significance the name might hold in the human tongue, but he mulled it over in his mouth. *Vic-to-ria.* It had a regal feeling. Who was he? He had to learn more of these humans.

His thoughts were interrupted as a server meekly placed a platter between Bargult and Best Wishes before scuttling away so quickly that its legs became tangled in a chair as it retreated. All mystery as to where they had gotten the meat vanished as Bargult picked up half a carcass and bit into it, cracking ribs between his jaws and prying off the meat. Cleaned and cooked, it was still not difficult to recognize the torso of one of the many different species he had counted along his trip through what he'd mentally dubbed the hollow. A juvenile, from the size of it.

Eating the flesh of sentient beings was not a practice within the Praetory but neither was it banned outright. The lesser empires were barely above animals at any rate, and it had been months since he had tasted real meat. Best

Wishes' stomachs rumbled as he reached for the steaming platter.

"Tell me of these humans," he said.

Bargult began to speak despite continuing to eat. However he was producing the sound it was not through his mouth. *"Scavengers, picking across the bones of star runners and disappearing into the void. They are prey, swift, deadly, and rare,"* he said.

Best Wishes' savored a mouthful of meat. It was overcooked, poor quality, likely incompatible with his biochemistry, and absolutely delicious. Above all, Dirregaunt were carnivores, and it had been months since he last had the taste in his mouth. Deep space missions involved a great deal of protein rations, but few meals with meat. He looked across at Bargult, who was cleaning blood off his face by scraping his mandibles across his jaws. "You give them too much credit, Grah'lhin Bargult. They do not face the Salvesei or any of the lesser empires. They have drawn the attention of the Dirregaunt, who have hunted across the stars for millennia, halted Malagath expansionism, and held back the Kossovoldt."

"And yet you have not seen their like. The humans are as ghosts. They are unpredictable, disappearing at will, striking without warning with weapons none can sense. They walk the void between ships and they speak all languages."

Best Wishes waved a hand dismissively. It was only when Bargult growled that he realized that the gesture bore resemblance to shooing an insect away. Perhaps seen as an insult between the Grah'lhin?

"I am not interested in hearsay and fanciful tales of space walkers. I need to know where the human planets are."

"None know where the human planets lay, only that they

are few in number and far from here. The human range far exceeds their fields. But you do not need to know. Human Victoria is not going home."

"No? Where then?"

"To know your prey you must know their habits. You well know this. When the humans come upon a wreck with survivors they ferry them home. It is not known why. Aboard Taru Station they took on stores compatible with Malagath digestion systems. I saw them myself as I hunted them through the caverns. They make for the Malagath frontier."

Best Wishes cursed, "There are thousands of stars spread between here and the Malagath territory."

"Yes, but many of them hostile, or incapable of reaching with the human engines. I know what path they take, and I will share it with you for an exchange."

"We can provide material compensation."

The Grah'lhin stabbed a spear-like foreleg through the remainder of the carcass and into the top of the composite table.

"Victoria is my quarry, hunter. I have no interest in material wealth, I want her on this table between us. I would be there when you run her down. Aboard your star runner and mine. I would share one more meal."

Best Wishes' rightmost eye tracked a small rivulet of blood creeping from the puncture. The other three focused on the monstrosity seated across from him, though seated was perhaps not the proper term. The Grah'lhin was apparently some sort of captain among his kind, but could he be trusted aboard the *Springdawn*?

Best Wishes leaned forward, baring his teeth. "Where has she gone, Grah'lhin Bargult?"

"Easy, Tessa. Take your time, line it up."

"Stuff it, Aimes, I know how to goddamn shoot," said Tessa. She relaxed. Aimes slipped into a teaching mode when he got nervous. It was good to know she wasn't the only one who was. She stared straight ahead as the feed on the tranquilizer attachment transmitted targeting video directly to her ocular implants. It was a tricky thing to learn, but you got used to it. The barrel of the attachment extruded just a few hairs breadth into the hangar that housed one of the Dirregaunt shuttles. She hoped the glare from the light fixture would be enough to hide it. Dirregaunt were said to have phenomenal senses, sight especially, all the way into the infrared range when they made use of a specialized eye. Something about their home planet's flora filtering the wavelengths on the surface differently depending on the season.

To Tessa it just made sense, The Dirregaunt were basically bony bipedal wolves with flattened faces and no noses. And about three times as many teeth. You'd have to be pretty thick to think they wouldn't have powerful vision and hearing. Hopefully it wasn't good enough to sense the diminutive report of the tranquilizer round.

She held her breath and squeezed, the receivers in her vacuum suit picking up the *piff* sound as the frozen needle of tranquilizer was pushed out on an expanding cushion of nitrogen. She hadn't even seen it go, and the Dirregaunt seemed not to notice it. She wondered if it had worked, the system had been sitting in storage for over a decade.

The lone Dirregaunt stopped its patrol, looked about, and then scratched at its hip where Tessa had been aiming. She grinned as it began to sway.

Aimes, also watching through the weapon's feed, let out a soft cheer and lowered the access hatch. He polarized the anchor for his auto-belay and dropped down on the thin carbon fiber ribbon, his own rifle trained on the Dirregaunt the entire time. As he landed Tessa clamped her own rider to the tether and slid down to land behind him, rifle covering the secondary airlock that led to Taru Station.

The Dirregaunt sentry blinked at him, then turned to stare at the stars through the translucent metal of the outer airlock. His portable maser hung forgotten on its lanyard.

"Look at him Tess. He's totally fried!" said Aimes as he let the ribbon retract. He would be able to pull it down again when it was time for them to leave.

Tessa had to agree, she hadn't expected to dart to work as well as it had. Unconscious bodies tended to draw unwanted attention, so the synthesized toxin was designed to devastate cognition and mnemonic functions without impairing motor skills. It was an induced blackout, and while it could see it could not properly comprehend or form new memories. The two Vultures were as ghosts.

She glanced over at Aimes, his neck craned to look at the towering shuttle. His voice crackled over her radio.

"Hell, Tess. It's almost as big as the *Condor*."

"Big Three don't much care about material constraints. Resource shortages are something that happen to other people. Their logistics limits are far surpassed by their manufacturing capability. And with their metals it's probably about a quarter the tonnage it looks."

"Yawn. Thanks for the xenosociology lesson. Let's find a way onboard, get that intel. Maybe even boost a part or two.

Tessa watched Aimes bound ahead, his rifle at the ready despite their recon confirming they had left only a single sentry. Hell, they hadn't even closed the ramp. She ran her hand over the underbelly of the shuttle, hoping to feel some measure of the texture through her glove. It was smooth as glass. She heard the metallic tromp of armored boots up the ramp and chased after it. Her heart had been icy cold and steady when she had taken the tranquilizer shot, now it raced, pounding in her chest. As far as she knew they were the first humans to set foot aboard a functioning Dirregaunt vessel. The Big Three didn't tend to dock in the same circles.

A hum of oscillating energy greeted her as she climbed the ramp, the suit's modest computer calculating its likely location within the shuttle. Her ocular implants lit up as they identified xenotechnology, but there was no library for what she was seeing. The Dirregaunt were so far ahead of them they couldn't even decipher a tenth of their technology, what little scraps humanity had scavenged over the years were still largely a mystery. The programming languages had been cracked, woefully underdeveloped as the Dirregaunt simply didn't need them. A team of specially trained crewmembers did astral calculations as precisely as any human computer.

"Aimes, you want bridge or engine room?" she asked. Aimes was already out of sight, damn if he wasn't right about this ship being almost the size of the *Condor*.

"Engine room, I want to see the look on Aesop's face when I tell him I rubbed my balls on a Dirregaunt horizon drive."

Tessa rolled her eyes and headed for the forecastle where she hoped to find the bridge. On the cruiser the command and control center would be deep within the ship, safe from piercing lasers and other weapons. It was the same way on the *Condor*. But on smaller ships and shuttles it wasn't uncommon to have the pilot's stations at the fore of the ship, behind a translucent alloy so that the navigator could guide by sight and feel instead of view screens.

The shuttle beyond the next hatch was surreal, hung with loose cables painted like vines and with swirling mist covering the deck. Tessa was suddenly feeling like she was back home in the Everglades on a cool morning, navigating the swamp with her grandfather's boat.

"Tess, you feel like you need a machete?" her radio chirped."

"You want another xenosocio lesson or you just like hearing yourself talk?"

"Oh please, Ms. Baum, take me to school. Learn me good," Aimes whispered in her ear. Tessa almost rebuked him, but reconsidered. Xenohistory and sociology was her passion and it was rare that she was given a chance to explore it. You generally didn't get into space without higher education but most marines opted for degrees in sports medicine or aviation or military science.

"The Dirregaunt home planet is a single band of swamp that wraps around their world from about 25° north to 50° south. That's why they've only got fur on their upper bodies, they spent a lot of time with their bottom halves submerged. Those bone hooks on their chest they'd loop over tree branches to sleep suspended out of the water until they learned how to build things to keep them above it."

"So the ship is like a marsh because of what, nostalgia?"

"Basically, yeah. It's easy to forget where you come from when you left your home planet eight millennia ago. By the time we were inventing things like pants, most of their race had never even seen their home world. The Praetory makes sure that their navy keeps their ships like this. Being back in a jungle helps them think like hunters, or at least that's the idea." said Tessa as she started up a ladder to the next deck. It made her feel like a gator was going to snap at her heels, between the mist and the vines it was too similar to the Everglades. Her retinal implants coordinated with her suit's computer, automatically mapping the interior and comparing it with Aimes' version. "I'm almost to the bridge," she huffed, finishing her climb.

The security was completely laughable, doors opened automatically as she approached, though she was unsure of the mechanism that sensed her passage. Of the labels on chambers she had seen nothing that read *armory* or *weapons locker*. A species at war in space for so long they had forgotten how to fight on the ground. It fascinated her. Pushing through the roiling mist on the deck she reached the hatch her implants insisted was the entrance to the bridge. It shimmered and slid open to accommodate her, rolling back like a liquid. She stepped through to the bridge.

Her retinal implants went crazy, highlighting control inputs, data displays, and translating the virtual HUD projected onto the translucent metal bow of the shuttle. She laughed as her vacuum suit's computer began synchronizing with the remote server a few decks up on Taru Station. A weekly crypto would be automatically sent in a few days as the server synched with the larger UE network, and with it, their data. If only this shuttle had a science station for her to ransack, but she would have to make do with the terminals displaying the precious engineering data. Her implants took snapshots as she scrolled down, stealing every numerical value they could detailing the operation of the Dirregaunt shuttle's engine.

"Hey Aimes, nothing sticky up here. How about the engine room? Anything not tied down?"

"Nah, everything is built right into the superstructure like a damned plastic mold. I grabbed what I think is an emergency respirator and maybe something to seal equipment breaches. Occs are going crazy back here though, I can barely keep track of everything. Tess, this is a gold mine, but we gotta get gone."

"That . . . may be a problem," Tess murmured into her radio as she ducked down.

Shit. Through the bow of the ship she could see the Dirregaunt returning to the hangar and approaching the stunned sentry. A *lot* of Dirregaunt. Looks like they were returning to the shuttle. The shuttle that just happened to have a pair of marines digging around inside. Had there been some sort of alarm they had tripped or did they just have rotten timing? They were five minutes into their seven minute planned excursion, and damn if they weren't the wrong seven minutes.

She heard Aimes swear as she opened up her ocular implant feed to show him the Dirregaunt detachment probing the stupefied sentry. No way out undetected. She used her virtual keyboard to pull up the partial schematic of the shuttle, frantically searching for another way out. There was none. They could shoot their way out, but if the Dirregaunt discovered there were still humans aboard Taru, and that they'd killed several sailors in their own hangar, they'd apply enough pressure to turn the entire station against them. They wouldn't be able to hide for an hour.

"Tess, what's the game?"

She highlighted an area of the schematics and sent the image to Aimes. "Here, meet me here, we just have to find a place to hide and hope they leave again soon. Quick, go now."

She abandoned the bridge, sliding down to the lower deck and meeting Aimes on the port side of the shuttle as her suit began to pick up the vibrations of the Dirregaunt boarding the craft. She pushed into what looked like berthing in front of Aimes, hoping that the Dirregaunt would have no reason to use the compartments on such a short trip. But where to hide . . . There were no bunks, Dirregaunt slept while suspended from hooks, a survival trait to put them out of reach to the primal predators of their primordial jungles. The lockers though. Inside? No, if they had any kind of shelving they'd never fit. Behind. There was some space between the bulkhead and the floor. She got down on her belly and squeezed into it, ceramic plating on the vacuum suit scratching a tiny groove on the back of the locker. Aimes slid in behind her, rifle held in his right hand in case they were discovered. All she could see was the ablative plating on his ass.

She saw Aimes tense up as the door slid open and a pair of footfalls began to pad inside. The rough whistling tones of the Dirregaunt language began to drift into her receiver and a translation appeared on her ocular implants.

"They said it looked as though he was drugged,"

"Tales. Low Branch is always sticking his nose where it is unwelcome. In this rotted hive it has given him more than he expected. He probably sampled the local fare. We are all likely to end up the same if we stay here any longer, I cannot believe the commander has struck a deal with one of them."

"I admit; Best Wishes is not as I expected. His pursuit of the Malagath Prince is . . . obsessive. Tavram is almost certainly dead."

"What can you expect of one born to the lower caste? He does not belong in command, and he will always have something to prove."

Tessa sighed. Some things were universal, bitching about your commanding officer appeared to be one of them. Her arm brushed against the bulkhead and she froze.

"Did you hear something?"

"Just the engine joining. Stow your gear and come."

Shit. Her suit had been reading new vibrations but she had hoped it wasn't the engine. Damn the luck. Aimes beside her was uttering a prayer. Funny, she never knew him to be religious, but it had the sound of something practiced. The deck shuddered beneath her belly as the shuttle spun away from Taru Station out towards space.

A questing hand brushed against hers and she clasped it wordlessly. Tessa was terrified, but she had her rifle, her vacuum suit, and most importantly a marine she'd fought beside for years. Behind the fear, though, she was surprised to find stubborn grit.

Ten thousand years ago the Dirregaunt had been a race of hunters, but despite the effort of the Praetory they'd left that behind when they spread across the stars. She had not. Let them see how humans hunted in the jungles. She squeezed her right hand and felt Aimes squeeze back.

"They're still after the *Condor*, Tess," he said.

"And they'll find her. Hell if they know where to look they can outrun her and be waiting. Marin doesn't have a prayer."

"No, but she has two marines already aboard the enemy ship."

"And we can cause nine kinds of hell. You think the Dirregaunt share the Malagath fear of space walkers?"

CHAPTER 6
CONFLICT OF INTEREST

"GOOD MORNING Miss Wong, Director Sampson is in your office."

Alice Wong paused, steaming coffee halfway to her lips.

"The Director? Did he say why?"

"No ma'am, only to send you straight in when you arrived."

Alice peered at the door behind her secretary, behind which the director of Union Earth Technology Division waited. Unusual for him to visit the State and Colonization department, UETD barely gave them the time of day. Everyone knew colonization was secondary to scientific and technological advancement. Half his time was spent in the offices of politicians across earth, the rest was spread between the various Union Earth research stations orbiting UE colonies that picked apart tech brought home by the Privateer Corps. He was one of a very select few individuals who warranted a personal ship equipped with a horizon drive. Alice Wong typically had to hitch a ride with a resupply freighter when she visited a colony.

Alice pushed the door open, the sharp click of her heels disappearing on the carpet. Director Sampson stood facing away from her, pensively looking at a photograph he removed from a shelf. She couldn't tell which one from her current angle. She approached.

"Alice, good morning. Please, come."

So it was *Alice* then, not, Miss Wong, or Madam Secretary. She was unsure whether to be complimented or insulted. His tone was quite familiar, despite having met her only once before, at the House of Parliament in London.

"Director Sampson," she said carefully. He smiled, but didn't correct her or offer her the use of his first name. So, he wanted to establish authority.

He raised the picture. "Your daughter?" He asked.

"Yes, Huian," she replied, "At her commissioning ceremony when she became an officer in the Navy." In the picture, Huian stood in her dress uniform, her new rank insignia being pinned to her collar. Alice had taken the picture herself, one of her proudest moments.

"Named for your late husband's mother, I see," he said. Retinal implants. Of course he would have them, like all the UEN and UEMC officers. And Huian too, now that she was a privateer. Alice set her tablet on her desk, feeling centuries behind.

Director Sampson continued. "Currently serving with the Vultures. Interesting coincidence. Have you met Captain Marin?"

Alice Wong had. She first encountered Victoria Marin at a christening ceremony whereby the woman got excessively inebriated and groped the assistant head of Colonial Affairs in front of his very scandalized wife. One did not readily forget Victoria Marin. She shuddered to think what habits Huian might be learning on the bridge of the *Condor* with her, but she had been switched at the last minute from the nice, safe Union Earth Navy billet Alice lined up for her.

"She struck me as a precocious woman, Director."

"She's an insufferable bitch is what she is. I feel badly for your daughter, stuck up there with that psychotic drunk. She should never have been given the *Condor*."

He raised a hand as if to run it through his silvering hair, but dropped it and replaced the photo. The plastic smile returned as he faced her, deepening the creases at the corners of his eyes.

"Actually the Vultures are the reason I'm planetside today. How well do you know Taru Station?"

"Taru? We have holdings there, managed by the Jenursa. Outside our normal support network but the privateers have had some success in that region. That whole area is a bit Wild West. Rowdy at the best of times."

"Rowdy is good, Alice. Rowdy means salvage. Rowdy means advancement for us. So rowdy, in fact, that the Vultures scuttled a Grayling vessel just off the station."

"What? When?" asked Alice. Her mind immediately went to Huian. She looked at the portrait Sampson had held earlier.

"Don't worry, your daughter is fine. It happened sometime last night, the *Condor* repelled an attack and hit back with a solid one-two that left the Grayling ship ballistic towards the first planet in the Taru System."

Alice let out a relieved breath, but paused. "That sounds like a privateer matter, what does it have to do with State and Colony?"

"Shrewd observation," countered Director Sampson, "The incident not so much, more about what they're hauling and what showed up after they hit the dusty before another couple cutters could warm up. Tell you what, it's easier just to show you. Why don't you pop open your terminal and take a look-see at your FTL cryptos?"

Alice glanced at her terminal, then back at the director, casually leaning against the wall with his arms crossed. He nodded toward the computer on her desk. Alice narrowed her eyes. How did Sampson know what was waiting on her crypto account? She circled around the desk, never taking her eyes off him.

The biometrics recognized her as she sat down, bringing up her personal interface. With practiced ease she navigated the several levels of security required to access the faster-than-light communications while Sampson waited. A flashing alert greeted her. She opened the message, scanned the contents, and gasped.

High Priority Hyperlight Dec 1st
Rec: Sec. Alicewong HT4776782
Send: Cpt. Vicmarin; PVTCondor TRU-STN
Advisement – ferryboat 10 heavy Malagath –
FP Tavram aboard pls. advise
Best time - Kallico'rey Malagath base 5 days,
hot salvage follows – tech Malagath pls. advise
Advisement – rspns PLM-STN.
Nd

Alice looked at the director in shock.

"The Malagath First Prince? Aboard the *Condor*? Good God I can't imagine the diplomatic nightmare Marin is going to conjure up!" she said. She buried her face in her hands, groaning. Sampson came and sat on the edge of her desk.

"It's a bit more complicated than that, Alice."

She looked up. "How could it be more complicated than Prince Tavram billeting on *that* privateer? You know the number of more important names in the known galaxy is down to the single digits, right?"

Sampson leaned forward. "Well, we have some friends owe us favors out that way that clarified the situation a bit. No, can't tell you how or why, but the skinny is that the ship they rescued the prince from is still on their tail. Now Victoria is tearing a streak across the sky trying to get him home 'fore the Dirregaunt cruiser on her tail, which she doesn't know about by the way, catches up."

"Director we have to warn them, give them a chance to make it to Kallico'rey," said Alice, for the moment concerned more for her daughter than with the depth of Sampson's intelligence data. She began preparing a response to send to the Pilum Forel listening post. A thick hand settled on her right wrist.

"Not so fast there, Miss Wong. Relax and take a deep breath."

"Relax? We have to get the First Prince off that ship, Director. It's a matter of state urgency."

There was that smile again, the one that narrowed his eyes. "Not entirely, Alice. Ordinarily, yes, rescues are matters for State and Colony. But in this case Victoria was mistaken in sending this crypto to you."

"Explain."

"Word in the stars is the Prince is set on negotiating a peace treaty between the Malagath Empire and the Dirregaunt Praetory. Something somewhere leaked and made someone unhappy."

"Peace between the Malagath and the Praetory? Think of all the lives that would be saved. Trade would go up, ideas would spread, and the Big Three might not vaporize everything in sight. God, it's hard to imagine being a part of that universe."

"Don't bother trying to imagine it. It's not a universe

the UE wants to be in."

"Excuse me?"

"It's simple, Alice. The UE runs on stolen tech. You can parade the Navy and the Union Earth Colonies around in front of congress and parliament and the Chinese president, but at the end of the day it's xenotechnology that keeps us in the black. It's xenotech that keeps us from getting scraped off the Orion Spur like a bad rash, and it's the Big Three tearing at each other's throats that provide us opportunities to salvage that xenotechnology."

"But most of our salvage doesn't even come from the Big Three, most of it is other xenos."

"War creates chaos, creates opportunities for opportunists, and creates desperate people that do desperate things. That chaos goes away and suddenly the galaxy becomes a lot more stable. The Big Three are then actually able to police their territories, proxy wars using the lesser empires become more infrequent, and human advancement dries up, and our progress slows to a crawl unless we start taking measures into our own hands."

Lesser empires. Lesser than whom? Humanity? Surely not, even Sampson couldn't be that arrogant. That was how the Big Three described, well, anyone who wasn't Big Three. Alice had just about enough.

"You want me to give the First Prince to the Dirregaunt cruiser. I won't do it."

Sampson frowned. "Alice, Alice, Alice. This isn't me asking. This is way over both of our heads."

"Then whoever is ordering it can draft the message, *and* sign it."

The director stood up again, walking to the window and looking up at the sky. The sun had yet to rise, and a few stars were still visible in the pre-dawn light.

"She's out there, you know. The fury of 10,000-year-old hunters is racing to devour her ship."

"Marin knows what she's doing."

"That's not who I was talking about."

Alice twisted away from the terminal.

Sampson clasped his hands behind his back and flashed a wolfish smile over his shoulder. "You don't think it was an accident that Huian was sent to the *Condor* instead of that cushy billet on the *Heinlein* do you? That she jumped to the front of the line in front of all those more qualified pilots with prior space time because she was the daughter of the SS&C? That takes a fair amount more clout than you have, Alice. It's a dangerous galaxy."

Alice Wong felt a chill creep through her blood. "What are you implying, Director?" she asked, standing.

Director Sampson took a deep breath, turned, and strode to the office door. "Send the damn crypto," he said, and closed the door behind him. Alice retrieved her tablet from the other side of the desk, and scanned it before sitting down once more at her terminal. She could not afford to hesitate.

"God forgive me," she whispered as she signed the First Prince's death warrant.

Would Captain Marin do the right thing?

CHAPTER 7
PILUM

Victoria sat alone in her stateroom, attempting to concentrate on her latest project by the light of a small lamp; A 23rd century UE destroyer, encased in a glass bottle. She should be sleeping. It had been almost two days since she had slept. Sleeping drugs never seemed to help her insomnia, and she couldn't drink until she passed out, not with the Malagath aboard. Hadn't stopped her completely though.

The tiny thruster she was setting fell over within the bottle, and she cursed, pushing away from the desk. The glass case containing the partially constructed model rolled over, fouling her work of the past half hour. She looked longingly at the bed, four hours still remained before the *Condor* arrived at Pilum Forel to request permission to transit the galactic territory of the Paralt. Four hours that she didn't want to spend lying in her rack staring at the blinking light of the command repeater. She tugged a fleece over her uniform and thumbed open the door to her stateroom. The whirring oscillation of the horizon drive greeted her, fueled by the exotic matter they managed to get aboard. Her ship still had its hurts. She had hoped to take a day or two at Taru to refit and repair, but now it looked like the *Condor* would be limping all the way to the Malagath frontier.

No drugs could make her sleep, but maybe seeing some of the engineering repairs would help. Yuri Denisov could make an atomic war sound dry. She passed the crew's lounge, wherein she spied two marines and a weapons tech teaching one of the Malagath to play Texas Hold 'Em. Probably cheating, too. She had expected the Malagath to isolate themselves within their quarters where the atmosphere had been modified to accommodate them, but was more than a little surprised to find that they were integrating themselves with the crew. The privateers of the *Condor* were no strangers to xeno life aboard her vessel, but the Malagath had a reputation for xenophobia and callous violence that made her assume they would enforce self-segregation. Maybe it was due to their interstellar form of feudal government. Individuals might not be as bad as officers, just trying to get by like the rest of them.

It took her only a few minutes to traverse the length of the *Condor* and enter the aft engineering bay crippled since the attenuator overloaded. Inside, her engineers labored to repair the damage with what material was on hand. Yuri Denisov was a deck down, working on the Gravitic Stealth Device. She descended to the lower level and found her chief wearing the far off expression of a man focused on reading his retinal implants. Not one for patience, Captain Victoria waved a hand in front of his face.

He started, focusing on her face.

"Vick, what brings you back to our neck of the woods? Horizon drive giving you migraines again?" Yuri asked. He looked somewhat worse for wear, Doc's handiwork showed where he had been burned following the attenuator's overload. A fairly serious burn, from the look of his bandages. His wide pupils gave away the presence of painkillers, and there was a slight slur to his voice. Victoria suspected this might be his last journey aboard the *Condor*, but he wouldn't leave while the ship was still hurt. He was one of the original Vultures, with her since she'd taken command.

"Just wanted to see how the repairs were coming along."

"Not as well as if we had another couple days at Taru, but damned if I want to bunk in a house with a Grayling. The Malagath make up for it, truth be told. Once they dumb down to our level, they soak up engineering know-how like a sponge. I never would have seen them helping us."

"They like knowing how things tick, us included. Don't think they wouldn't strip us apart as fast as any of your equipment if they had the chance. How's the GSD coming along?"

"Let me just asked my newest engineering team," said Yuri. He thumbed the engineering circuit on his console, "Cohen, bring the new gal up for a minute."

Victoria waited while Aesop Cohen ascended from the lowest level, helping one of the Malagath rescues up behind him. Her arm was in a sling. It looked like Doc Whipple had modified the medical gear to accommodate her. She approached behind Cohen, who saluted.

"Captain."

Victoria ignored him, eyeing the blue-skinned Malagath up and down. She met the eyes of the xeno, so possessing familiar intelligence and yet so alien. The spark of sentience was almost universal, at least for any xeno's possessing eyes, anyway. Victoria had often wondered if the rescues could detect the same thing, or if they saw her as little more than an animal.

"Yuri, I don't know if I like her futzing with the Gravitic Stealth Device. That's classified."

Her chief engineer laughed, "As if we had any secrets the Malagath hadn't forgotten before we climbed out of our caves. Aurea has already brought me a laundry list of improvements we can make to it."

The Malagath engineer stepped forward, "It's not all that dissimilar to the theory behind the emergency engine employed by the *Dreadstar* which brought us to your astral territory, Captain Marin," she volunteered, "Both devices adjust local space-time to create mass. Your device? Negative mass. Our device? Positive, enough mass to initiate a space tear, what your crew calls a horizon jump. Functionally very similar."

"Cohen?" asked Victoria.

"She's not wrong, Captain, from the way she's described it to me. I'll grant the Malagath version puts out about as much mass as a small star, but they only really maintain it for a fraction of a second."

"And we would never leave a calculation that important to a computer," added Aurea, still somewhat scandalized that a species would put such investiture in a technology the Malagath so readily dismissed millennia past as good only for opening doors and displaying documents. Victoria chuffed. *If they only knew*, she thought.

Victoria left before Yuri could launch into a technical tirade about the GSD, maneuvering her way past two marines on a pair of exercise bikes. Square feet were at a premium, so you shoved workout equipment wherever it could be strapped down. If it wouldn't jeopardize her command, she would invite one to exercise in her rack. UE protocol was explicit when it came to commanding officers bunking with their crew. Just fore of the engine room were the ship's command and control center, unmanned for the duration of the Horizon jump, and the sensor shack. The sensor shack usually maintained only a single operator when transiting between stars, but she could clearly make out the voice of Dan Avery, her senior sensor supervisor.

She slipped into the shack, careful not to disturb Avery or his two operators.

"You're sure there's nothing in the banks about it?" she heard him ask. Avery leaned against the operator's chair as he scanned the screen through his glasses, a cup of coffee steamed in his long-fingered hand. His hair was mussed, and his normally smooth face roughened with stubble. All in all, not a bad look for him, she thought.

Avery caught her reflection in the screen, and started, almost spilling his coffee over the sensor stack. "Vick, I was just trying to decide if this was worth waking you over."

She stepped further into the shack, greeted by the smell of hot circuitry and the rush of ventilation overhead. "Well I'm already awake, so you're not risking an ass-kicking. Now talk."

He sighed, rubbing the back of his neck with a slender hand. With the other he reached over the shoulder of his operator and brought up an unfamiliar screen on the sensor stack.

"It's probably nothing, but Joyce picked up a . . . well, I'm not sure what to call it. Horizon space backwash maybe?"

On the screen was a jumble of red lines, relatively flat, except for a single bump, barely above its neighbors, which Avery panned over and enlarged.

"Theoretically this should let us detect shifts in mass leaving horizon space. Like tossing a rock into a pond and picking up the ripples. Here's the rock," he said pointing to the peak. He moved his slender finger down the wave, "and here's the ripple. Barely above background levels, all things considered. But to make any kind of splash you've got to be either fast, heavy, or both. We're talking on the order of thousands of tons. But we've never had any kind of indication of other ships leaving horizon space before, we're the test bed for this platform."

Victoria clenched her fists and looked away from the screen. "What's the bearing?"

"Pilum Forel. What do you think it could be? Bulk merchant freighter?"

"Nothing good. Damn, there's only a dozen xenos fielding that kind of tonnage. No way it's coincidence."

"Maybe it's a Malagath ship and we can hand over the First Prince and his crew?"

Victoria shook her head, "Not a chance, the range on those ships makes stopping at Pilum Forel pointless, they can just jump right past the system.

So much for sleep.

She dialed her XO's stateroom into the growler, buzzing him awake.

"XO," he muttered. Unlike Victoria, horizon space put him right in the rack. It affected everyone slightly differently.

"Carillo, nap's over. Pilum may be hot when we get there, get the ship ready."

Her executive officer gave a groggy aye-aye before she cut the connection.

Avery might be right, could be nothing. Or it could be a bulk freighter. It wouldn't be unusual, Pilum Forel was a heavily trafficked system. Or there could be a Dirregaunt battleship waiting for them, to finish what they started. The only way to find out was to keep going. Besides, there was no way to turn back. Horizon space jumps were a one-way trip. Hopefully ferrying the First Prince wouldn't turn out to be the same way.

Best Wishes gazed at the binary stars through the primary view screen aboard the *Springdawn's* bridge. Pilum, the lesser, and Forel, the greater, as the locals called them. The lesser empires used this system as a travel hub. Pilum was possessed of rare properties which made it shine brightly in horizon space, casting a wide net across the cosmos to ensnare captains who aimed for her. Forel had such stability that it eased the burden of the calculations required and extended a vessel's safe range. A short transit between the two might cut days off of a journey and conserve the precious catalysts required to slip into the space behind space. The binary system changed hands many times, as a beacon of economic and strategic importance. Currently the lesser empire of the Paralt claimed ownership, and charged a handsome fee to organizations wishing to make use of the binary system's advantages. How did any of these freighters turn a profit when everywhere they turned they encountered trade tariffs and docking fees?

A Dirregaunt battleship paid fees to no one, least of all the lesser empires, and the garrison at Pilum Forel scrambled to acquiesce to the dictates of the *Springdawn's* commander. If the primordial terrors that were the Grah'lhin had steered him correctly, this *Human Victoria* would enter at Pilum within an hour, and request transit to Forel, which they would use to continue on towards the Malagath front. Or so he was to believe.

Best Wishes held small trust for the Grah'lhin. It stood, pensive, on the raised observation ring, often not moving or reacting to stimuli. It claimed that others of its kind were on their way, though how it communicated with them was a mystery. His crew offered a wide berth to the creature wherever it went.

Best Wishes was still scrutinizing the creature when

Earthen Musk burst through the gate to the bridge, stumbling up to his first officer. Modest Bearing looked up, catching Best Wishes' eye. A worried look adorned his face, his teeth bared just so. The sensory tips in Best Wishes' mane started to itch, those vestigial organs evolved to sense the wind of predators. This was not the time for trouble, not with their prey less than an hour away.

Modest Bearing approached, the runner in tow, but once again refusing to meet Best Wishes' eyes.

"Commander, I think you will want to see this for yourself, but one of our own is dead, killed outside the shuttle bay."

"Who? And how?" demanded Best Wishes, directing the question at Earthen Musk.

The runner looked uncomfortable as he answered. "Lightest Grove, her mate witnessed it. He's near catatonic. He said . . . he said it was space walkers."

An ancient superstition, beings that walked through space and haunted those who traversed the stars. They were a myth, a legend even. How could she be dead? Best Wishes would have to see the still blood within her veins through his top eye to believe it.

A heavy thump behind him and the frightened recoils of his crewmates caused him to glance back. The Grah'lhin was once again active, and lumbering towards them. Its forelegs collapsed, bringing its slick sensory band level with Best Wishes as the protective carapace slid away. Moist, shiny mandibles clicked to either side of a nightmare mouth, and Best Wishes resisted the urge to step away.

"*You will go to look upon this fallen Dirregaunt?*" asked Bargult, his chittering voice so deep it almost blended with the engines.

Best Wishes grimaced. "If there is a fallen Dirregaunt.

I'm not given to fanciful tales of space walkers."

The giant insect resumed its full height. Its wings buzzed softly within the confines of its carapace. "*I would look upon her as well,*" it affirmed.

"Master hailman, contact the Paralt. Tell them to be prepared to receive the human vessel. And summon Measured Calm, if he has not already been. His expertise will be required to enlighten us as to the true nature of our sister's death. And to absolve these foolish notions of . . ." he eyed Earthen Musk, who shrunk beneath his gaze. "Space walkers."

"Yes, Commander."

"Very good. First Lieutenant, you have the bridge."

Best Wishes made his way back toward the shuttle bay, through the hydroponic jungle and induced fog which the Praetory believed kept the Dirregaunt grounded in their planetary history. To traverse the length of the *Springdawn* would take perhaps a quarter hour, but the shuttle bay resided amidships, just aft of the center of gravity and the habitation chambers. Upon entering the compartment, onlookers cleared from his path while his medical crew examined the body. It was unmistakably Lightest Grove, she had a distinct pattern of spots on her shoulders. Blood hung in the air, teasing his mane, and it wasn't hard to see why. Several holes had been torn in Lightest Grove's torso, great ragged things that had sprayed the foliage with her life's blood.

Bargult tried to approach the body, but at a grunt from Best Wishes, his crew moved to block him. A security team was present, their weapons raised a twitch before checking themselves. He didn't want the thing profaning her with its proximity. He had half a mind the Grah'lhin intended to devour the body. Six long legs turned the monstrosity toward him, swinging the bulk of the matte black body. "*What do you smell, Dirregaunt Best Wishes?*" it asked.

"Blood, death. Fear from the crew. Dirt, and the fiber of the vines above."

"What *else*?"

Best Wishes focused on the olfactory nodes in his mane. There was something, brushing against them ever so slightly, teasing them, switching the tips of his receptors. A sulfurous odor, like an acid bath. And . . . smoke? Combustibles?

Bargult gestured to the body. "*The wounds are as living flesh, yes? No burns, nor scoring of the meat?*"

That *meat* had been part of his crew. Best Wishes suppressed a wave of revulsion. Measured Calm had beaten them to the shuttle bay. He looked up from the body, visibly sickened by the ordeal. "There is not, my Commander. No plasma burns, no particle scoring, no irradiated inflammation. It's as though she was killed by air."

The wings chittered again, the buzz grating his nerves. Best Wishes held no desire to draw closer to the body, yet the only witness to the deed, Broad Resolve, knelt cradling his mate's head. The whistling keen of his mourning song filled the hollow chamber. Best Wishes approached, kneeling beside the body.

"Who did this? Who has taken her from us?" he asked.

"She went to check the shuttles, and when she opened the airlock, they were waiting. They were the void. Two, the purest black of the space between stars, they carried the thunder of storms. I . . . Oh dear Praetor I can still hear their echo. Make it stop, *make it stop.*"

Best Wishes drew back as the crewman's recounting devolved into a howl of primeval terror and loss. Security officers moved to restrain him, but Broad Resolve simply collapsed over his mate once again. The engineer was mad, his mind shattered by the trauma of the long service and witnessing the death of his mate. He would find a new place to call home, on one of the many planets beneath the Praetory's canopy. But his service in space was over.

Best Wishes prepared to remand him to the sick bay for a sedative to dispel, this notion of space walkers, but stopped. How would he react were it Dutiful Heiress on the deck? Broad Resolve had crafted a demon of his own imagination to blame. Creatures that walked through the black of space outside the safe hulls of the Praetory haunted the nightmares of the Dirregaunt, Malagath, and Kossovoldt for millennia. Each had their variation on the tale. And yet, something killed her. Something he could not explain.

"What say you of space walkers, Dirregaunt?"

The Grah'lhin had spoken softly, bringing Best Wishes back to the present. The story of space walkers was just that, a story to scare children. He stood, turning to regard the Grah'lhin.

"There is no such creature. All who enter the void perish."

Again, the chittering wings. Best Wishes began to realize the noise as an indication of amusement. He was tempted to crack open that shell and tear the wings off the disgusting creature. How dare he disrespect the death of his crew before her widower.

"Pray, do you find something about this funny, Grah'lhin Bargult?" he demanded, teeth bared, claws sliding forward on his fingers.

"The irony, Dirregaunt. We lay in wait for the humans, yet did I not tell you? The humans are as ghosts. They are already aboard your ship."

"Impossible," said Best Wishes, rejecting the

implication. It made no sense, they had arrived at Taru only after the human ship had already left. Or so Bargult claimed. Were it not for the alien's familiarity with the elements of his crewmate's death, he would have Grah'lhin Bargult removed from the bay. He showed an intimacy with the details that spoke of his experience hunting them. But it was little better an explanation than space walkers. They hadn't even docked at Taru.

But the shuttles had.

Another runner arrived, pausing before Best Wishes to regain his wind. The commander of the *Springdawn* didn't need to hear his message to know what news he brought. Humans may or may not have been aboard his ship. That was yet to be determined.

But they were most certainly in Pilum Forel.

CHAPTER 8
FOREL

THE HARSH, MIND-BENDING blue-white shapes of horizon space flashed to the black matte of the stellar scape on the primary view screen of the *Condor*. The star, Pilum, dominated the port side of the ship, spiking radiation sensors along the level azimuth. In the distance, Forel burned softly, the only other star visible in the sky while the binary pair were in view.

Victoria stood behind Huian, all her command displays within easy reach. She had repeaters for sensors, weapons, navigation, and engineering feeding her details about the *Condor's* current status. From the ablative plating to the xenon-powered engines she could call up any information she wished. And behind her, First Prince Tavram once again occupied the XO's chair.

Activating the general circuit, Victoria cleared her throat and addressed the crew.

"This is the Captain, we have reentered normal space and are en route to Forel. From now until jump, battle stations are to remain manned and ready. There's no certainty the *Springdawn* is here, but I didn't get to be an old iron bitch by getting caught with my pants down," she said. Perhaps not the most accurate turn of phrase, since she had been caught just so on several occasions, often by someone's wife.

She closed the circuit, and addressed her sensor team on the open microphone.

"Avery, what have you got for me?"

"Entry was smooth, but the Paralt picked up on it right away. I've got a carrier a half million klicks out. Two fighters inbound, within visual range. No hails yet." A subdivision of the main screen showed the two sleek fighters, cruising in, beginning to decelerate a few dozen kilometers away. They flew at a ninety-degree cant from the *Condor's* perspective. While the human fleets oriented themselves parallel to the local stellar plane, the Paralt method of orientation held the local star as down, and the stellar plane more of a stellar hamster wheel.

Damned fast, even for the Paralt's comparatively advanced sensors. She had debated climbing out of the stellar plane, maintaining full dark all the way to Forel. But if they were caught, the Paralt would blast them out of the sky without word or a second thought. Not big on trespassers who tried to avoid transit fees, were the Paralt.

"Incoming data-link request, Vick. Standard comm protocols."

Victoria thumbed her console, switching one of her screens to show the interior of the fighter hailing her. Within, the pilot was fully enclosed in his suit, his narrow, wedge-shaped helmet betraying his alien anatomy. He was treated to a similar view of her. He moved jerkily in the low-resolution camera.

"Unidentified ship, you have entered Paralt territory. Declare yourself and your intentions, and present your benefactor code if you possess one."

"This is Captain Victoria Marin, of humanity's *UEP Condor*. Our intentions are to transit to Forel for a jump.

We are sponsored by the Jenursa, sending the authorization code now."

The video com cut out. There was a pause, longer than she liked, before the pilot came back on with his response.

"Very well, Human Victoria. The Jenursa accounts are in good standing and you are cleared to transit via the Forel six-two standard procedure. Maintain subluminal speeds within Pilum Forel."

The deviant procedure was hardly strange in and of itself. It could just mean the Paralt were seeing heavy traffic through the system. But Victoria didn't like all the little things stacking up, not with such precious cargo.

"Huian, plot the procedure and take us to point-seven. It's 40 AU's to the closest Forel jump point."

"Aye ma'am, plotting now. Estimated time to horizon jump is seven hours," said Huian. The hum of the Alcubierre drive began to drone through the hull of the ship. Typically used for faster-than-light maneuvers, it also significantly cut down on the time it took to accelerate at sublight speeds compared to the *Condor's* primary engines. But it also left almost no room for maneuverability, the risk of compression shear was too great.

"Sensors to the conn," came Avery's voice. He appeared a moment later, no longer bedraggled and unshaven. He approached Victoria's sensor repeater, bringing up the passive display.

"Here's what we've got so far, Vick. Liners, cargo, a couple smaller ships. If the *Springdawn* is here, then she's dark. What we've got on the Dirregaunt favors ambush tactics."

"So don't expect much warning before they take their first shot. And you can bet the Paralt will be giving them all the information they goddamned need. Violating their own neutrality pact, but I can't blame the fuckin' cowards if they've got a Dirregaunt battleship breathing down their necks. We'll have to be ready to cut the Alcubierre and switch to maneuvering engines. We're floating shit-scrap on a predictable compression course, especially subluminal. The Dirregaunt can work out a firing solution from a half-million klicks. Avery, I need to know the second you get a whiff of them."

"Aye skipper."

Victoria turned back to the main view screen, where the star, Forel, slowly began to enlarge as they accelerated to seven tenths of the speed of light. In saving the First Prince of the Malagath Empire she had made an enemy of the Dirregaunt. Were they out there, even now? Or was she worried over nothing?

———

"Tess, the engines."

Tessa boosted the audio sensors on her vacuum suit. Around them, lights in the massive chamber began to dim, casting the forested interior of the *Springdawn* into an artificial twilight. What passed for trees to the Dirregaunt began to give off a soft phosphorescent glow that highlighted the marks where the panicked Dirregaunt had scratched her ablative plating before Aimes shot it almost five hours ago. They meant to sneak off the shuttle, but the only thing sloppier than getting caught and killing one of the Dirregaunt was leaving the second one alive. Now the crew knew there was a hostile presence aboard the *Springdawn*, if not the precise nature of it.

They had been avoiding armed patrols for several hours. Luckily the ship was so enormous and the plant life so dense that the crew had trouble policing it, and two small humans were easily lost as they mapped the interior of the vessel. Their ocular implants were constantly ping-ing new data to their suits' onboard computers, data that would never be useful to the Union Earth.

"You think that's for us?" asked Aimes as the Dirregaunt reactors continued to spool down. But Tessa knew it wasn't. Their access to intel was limited, but they had picked up some chatter from the crew of the *Springdawn*. They were waiting for Captain Marin and the *Condor*. The Dirregaunt were ambush predators, attempting to reduce the chance their ship might be picked up by passive sensors by power-ing down non-essential systems. The darkening bay meant the *Condor* must be close, and yet, unreachable. Taru Sta-tion felt like a lifetime behind.

She remembered watching the *Condor* soar towards the star at the center of the system, in her head she could still hear the final radio chatter from the privateer ship, the background hum of the *Condor's* engines behind it, be-fore finally going out of range. How far had that been? A hundred thousand klicks? Two? Radios had come a long way ever since humanity gained access to xeno transceiv-ers. Would the *Condor* pass within radio range before the *Springdawn* launched its attack? Within the range of the *Springdawn's* communicators, certainly. They could broad-cast further than they could shoot, on the order of millions of kilometers, at the very least.

What if they could use that equipment? What if they could somehow warn the *Condor* using the communica-tion system on the Dirregaunt battleship? Shit, would they even know the comms gear if they were looking straight at it? The flora belied the advanced nature of the ship. The composite flooring looked like topsoil, but hardened when pressure was applied. The doors were almost like a liquid, sections turning transparent before sliding open entirely without hinges or apparent mechanisms. Most obvious tech they'd stopped to examine came back with three or four likely possibilities. Even the lighting filtering down through the red canopy seemed to mimic a star's path across the sky, without any apparent light source once you climbed above it. But how alien could a radio room look? Thus far, anything with an interface had proved little problem for them, the suit computers were excellent at handling any required inputs, and humans had encountered Dirregaunt computers before. *Only good for opening doors, turning on the lights, and warning humanity of impending death and disaster.*

"Hey boy, it's getting late. What say we give Mommy a call?" said Tessa, eyes on Aimes through the hard shell of her helmet. She saw Aimes pause for a moment before following her line of thought. Smart kid, boarding tactics had been his area of focus. Plotting and running scenarios to invade hostile craft had been a passion since she'd known him. It was probably why they hadn't been caught yet. He stilled, pulling up whatever schematics he could find on his suit's data drive similar to the ones he'd been building. A moment later Tess received a file-share request. She accepted, and her ocular implants began to fill with drawings and computer generated plans.

"Obviously we don't have an exact layout for a Dirregaunt Dreadnought," said Aimes, "but this ain't the first time we seen one, either. Closest I can compare to what we've got are some of the fourth-gen hulks."

A Praetor-class cruiser design appeared in her vision, a subsection outlined in red. "Here's the communication hub for the fourth-gen cruiser. But here," said Aimes as another diagram came up side by side with the first, "is a Hawk-class. See the communications hub is further aft along the dorsal? Here's what we've got on the *Springdawn*."

A third image displaced the first two, an incomplete profile view of the ship, with likely areas filled in by their mapping algorithm. Two compartments along the dorsal ridge of the ship were highlighted.

"Two possible spots," she whispered.

"Well, hundreds of *possible* spots. Hell, we don't even know if it's dorsal on this class, except that we saw the external equipment there. But if I were betting, here's where I'd put my money."

"To hit both we'll have to split up," said Tessa. She didn't like it as soon as she said it. It was easier for a wide search to find two people apart than two together.

"Every problem is an opportunity. Here, catch."

She looked up in time to see Aimes toss a small canister her way. She caught it, looking at the cylindrical profile of the exotic matter grenade. Tessa brought her gaze back up to matte black faceplate of Aimes' vacuum suit. She could imagine him grinning behind it. And a smile crept onto her own face as she guessed what he would say next.

"I'll take the forward compartment, you take aft. You get there and it don't look like comm gear, blow the shit out of it, raise hell, and get out quick."

"Quicker than greased lightning. You know this is likely to be a one-way ticket."

"Aw hell, we were dead the moment we set foot on that shuttle, and you know it. 'Sides, what are two marines against everyone on the *Condor*? You know what the Major would do if it were him here."

Aimes climbed to his feet, picking up his rifle from the tree he it leaned against and reattached it to his magnetic sling. He drew close to Tessa, and cupped a gloved hand to the side of her helmet. Her eyes stung as she leaned into him, two black panes of composite armor preventing her from touching him one last time.

"You know boy, only two or three guys I'd rather storm a Dirregaunt battleship with," she said.

"Yeah, but how many of them love you like I do?"

"None," she said softly.

Aimes pulled away. Tessa picked up her own rifle as she watched him disappear into the thick fog of the artificial forest.

"See ya 'round, Tess."

Best Wishes stood, transfixed by the main view screen. His claws clicked against the bone protuberances on his chest. The human ship was nearly within range of the *Springdawn's* forward-firing lasers. The course the Paralt ordered them to follow would take them within a light-second of the second planet, behind which the *Springdawn* waited. His engines were powered down to minimize the risk of detection, only the sensors and the capacitors for his weapons remained energized. Mere moments separated him from his prey now, and Prince Tavram would not escape again.

A low rumble translated through the floor paneling, vibrating his command console and briefly distorting the view screen's display. He dug his claws into the sides of his station to remain on his feet. *What was that?* Alarms began to sound on the bridge. The frequencies for both explosion and decompression alarms overlapped but his careful hearing easily differentiated them. He looked to his first officer.

"Commander, loss of integrity in the forward sensor array. The crew reports they heard . . . thunder before the explosion."

Best Wishes' pulse began to quicken. Broad Resolve had heard thunder when his mate was killed. Oh, Praetory, *Dutiful Heiress was assigned to forward sensors.* "Dispatch security teams to all adjacent compartments. Man the doors, I am coming myself."

"What of the *Condor*?"

"Fire as soon as we have a solution," Best Wishes replied, already halfway to the door of the bridge. He cursed under his breath when he felt, more than heard, the Grah'lhin following behind. Members of the security team began to flank him, one offering a handheld laser to Best Wishes.

The team reached the boundary of the area affected by decompression. Six compartments adjacent to the forward sensor array had been affected All those within were almost certainly dead. They would have to remotely seal the doors to isolate the sensor array. The hiss of air caused the entire security team to flinch around him.

"My Commander," said the young lieutenant of his security force, "The chamber is repressurizing."

As if he didn't already know. "Has the remote system been accessed?" he asked.

"Not by us."

Then what? "Steady, hunters," said Best Wishes. The hiss of moving air drew down, and he felt the security team tense up as the lock on the door cycled by itself. *Not by itself, by something on the other side.* By the Praetor, the deck had been exposed to vacuum, something could have gotten in.

No, he wouldn't fall prey to superstition. He wouldn't! He was better than that. Better. A hollow creak echoed through the room as the damaged door began to slide open. Thick gray smoke poured through the crack, smelling sickly sweet. There was more blood in the air. He focused his top eye, attempting to pierce the smoke and see beyond the visible spectrum of his primary eyes. There were strange particulates in the smoke, like flecks of metallics blocking most of even his infrared gaze. And behind it, something colder than the smoke. Something . . . vaguely bipedal.

His security lieutenant saw it too. He fired into the smoke, the rest of his team following suit. Lasers clicked and hummed as capacitors were discharged and refilled, creating a brilliant display through his fourth eye. The smoke flared as the lasers' energy dissipated within. The . . . *thing*, remained on the other side, one arm strangely much longer than the other. It raised that arm towards the door.

Not longer, realized Best Wishes, *holding something.*

"Lieutenant, get down!" shouted Best Wishes as he dove to the decking. Thunder filled the compartment, painful to his highly sensitive ears. The security lieutenant hit the deck next to him, sightless eyes staring above a pair of steaming holes in the lieutenant's face. Beyond the lieutenant, another of the security team gurgled as blood wept between the fingers he held over his throat. Best Wishes shouted at him, but his ears had drawn themselves shut to avoid further damage to their sensitive inner organs.

The cold thing, he refused to call it a *spacewalker,* slid out of the smoke. It was black, and definitely bipedal. Slightly shorter than a Dirregaunt. It had no face, but Best Wishes could feel its regard. Before it could act he felt the lumbering roar of the Grah'lhin translate through the flooring under his hands, and saw the things attention snap up as the giant insect charged. It raised the artifact in its hands again, the tip flashing brightly as it strafed away from the Grah'lhin. Something severed two of Bargult's legs, and sent shattered chips of carapace spinning away. Best Wishes made an attempt with his laser, but succeeded only in briefly warming the surface of the cold thing before it vaulted over him and out the door by which the security team had arrived.

Spacewalker. There could be no doubt. It had come in through the hull breach. Was this a human? How many were on the *Springdawn*? The rest of the security team watched, dumbfounded. He barked them to their feet, ordering their pursuit. His ears were opening back up, and he could hear the thunder retreating through the compartments ahead. A few spirited remarks had them pursuing the terror through the dorsal forests of the *Springdawn*.

Overhead the lights dimmed further, and a hum vibrated through the ship. The human ship had passed into range, and his first officer, Modest Bearing, had taken the shot. A moment passed. Then the engines began to spool up, and the forward capacitors whined as charge flowed into them. The *Springdawn* prepared for a chase and a second shot. *They had missed.* Best Wishes threw the laser to the ground, smashing it beneath a powerful, clawed foot, again and again, until components began to tear bloody gouges in the skin of his pads. He had no words to describe his anger, so he simply screamed, silent to his own ears, deaf to the thunder of the retreating spacewalker.

"Huian, cut the compression. Bring us to point two while we're within the planet's gravity well."

"Aye ma'am."

Forel Beta, the second planet orbiting their destination star grew rapidly on the view screen as the Alcubierre drive was secured, restoring the *Condor* to her primary maneuvering engines. Their assigned procedure vectored them between the planet and its first moon, a distance slightly greater than a light second. Passing between opposed celestial forces under the effects of compression was unpredictable at best, and had sheared more than one ship into scrap metal with all hands still aboard.

"I don't like this. Huian, deviate twelve degrees south azimuth. Let's see how itchy the Paralt are."

The view of the planet shifted on the primary screen as the *Condor* tilted to a nose-down attitude relative to the solar plane. Her communications console buzzed immediately. She thumbed the circuit, bringing up the pilot of another fighter assigned to shadow them.

"Paralt interceptor, *Condor,* deviating from course to avoid debris field in orbit above the planet, will resume course when clear of hazard."

"Negative, *Condor,* my scope is clear. Check your sensors and resume assigned course immediately to maintain traffic separation."

Victoria looked at her sensor repeater, showing the bearings and distances to all traffic in the area offered up by Avery and her sensor team. Liners, cargo hulks, and small, speedy envoy craft cluttered her queue, none of which was close or marked as a contact of interest. In fact, this entire quadrant of the system seemed clear. Except for what looked like . . . a human friend-foe identifier?

"Uh huh . . . listen champ, I'll get back to you, I have another call," she said. Not like he had anything useful to say anyhow. She cut off the interceptor's reply, switching to the strange broadcast. It was weak, likely a bounce signal. Maybe off the moon.

". . . *imes Webb of the . . . anyone r-r-receiving . . . ing-dawn ambush imminen—*"

Ice poured down Victoria's spine into every nerve in her body.

"Huian, punch it, *now!*"

Victoria was pressed back into her command couch as the *Condor* accelerated faster than her gravitic dampeners could compensate. Light washed out her rear view screen as the *Springdawn's* deep-space lasers tore through the space the *Condor* had occupied only moments earlier. The computer had no origin, the lasers had come from behind the planet, refracted through the upper levels of the atmosphere. The math involved in such precision staggered Victoria, humanity might as well be cavemen compared to the Dirregaunt. *Apex ambush predators.* Hell, humanity wasn't even on the food chain.

Alarms blared across the bridge as the Dirregaunt ship passed into view.

"Conn, sensors, Dirregaunt contact, two-nine-two, distance three-forty K-K. Profile indicates it's the *Springdawn.*"

"Yeah, no shit Avery, I got that. Give me something useful. Huian, initiate an evasion program, distance one light-second. Get us to Forel."

As she spoke, the broadcast entered direct line-of-sight, clearing up.

"*Say again, Marine Aimes Webb of the Condor, to any human forces in this system, anyone receiving, Springdawn attack is imminent.*"

"Thanks Webb," Victoria whispered. She couldn't pretend to know how he had managed to get the *Springdawn* to broadcast a warning of its own ambush, but damned if that boy hadn't saved the ship."

"Conn, sensors. Looks like the *Springdawn* was mostly shut down for the ambush, we've got a few seconds max before she's back online."

A few seconds could buy a lot of time, the *Condor* already had a few hundred thousand kilometer lead, but the

Springdawn had a technological edge by the order of several magnitudes, like a tactical Alcubierre drive that could shunt them around faster than the speed of light. But they hadn't engaged it.

"Avery, why haven't they gone superluminal to chase?"

"Spectrum shows gas particulates along the dorsal hull, I think they have a hull breach. They're picking up speed though, Vick. Best estimate is five minutes until they're back in range. Takes a lot to move a ship that big. Those interceptors are a bigger problem, my scope shows an intercept course one-fifty K-K and closing."

"They're just trying to make a good show for the Dirregaunt. Tac, send a few dummies their way, give em an excuse to break off the hunt."

The ship bucked twice as a pair of missiles shot away, screaming toward the approaching interceptors. On her repeater, she watched the two small fighters change course to retreat. That should keep the Dirregaunt off the Paralt's back.

"Ma'am, should we engage the Alcubierre? With the *Springdawn* unable to enter a compressive state we could outrun them."

"Negative Huian, we don't know for sure they can't, only for sure that they're catching up now. We slip into a compression and maybe they decide to risk it, or maybe they plan to take advantage of our blindness to sweep around and get ahead of us. Don't underestimate how clever xenos are. Just squeeze every ounce of acceleration you can out of the main engines."

It still might not be enough. By her math was another 8 minutes to the jump shell at their current speed. The Dirregaunt only needed a few seconds to line up a shot, but they needed to close to within a light second to reliably overcome the ship's evasion protocols. Or they could get lucky and turn the *Condor* into scrap.

There was still one more trick she could try, while they were out of the *Springdawn's* visual range.

"Tac, detach the gravitic buoy. Huian, twelve degrees up azimuth. Yuri, engage the GSD and drop the heat shield."

The gravitic buoy was an expensive little toy, able to fool most of the gravitic and heat sensors the xenos employed. Victoria had no idea whether it would work on the Dirregaunt, but the GSD had kept them hidden before, or so she thought. After all, the *Springdawn* had found them in a system the Dirregaunt had no other reason to be in. She watched as the *Condor's* ballistic course took them further from the trajectory of the buoy. The gravity on the *Condor* remained steady, even as the tones of her ship changed.

"Yuri, why am I not floating? Gravitic stealth status?"

"The GSD is fully functional, captain. That Malagath engineer has been making improvements to our designs. You wouldn't believe the stuff she's been cooking up back here."

Well, at least they were good for something. Less risk of losing her lunch in the microgravity.

"Conn, sensors. *Springdawn* remaining on present course, no alteration."

"It looks as though your gambit has succeeded once again," said the First Prince behind her. Victoria nearly jumped, she had forgotten Tavram was even there.

"We're not out of the fire yet, your royal princeness," she said, turning to his steady regard. No emotion showed on his face, though they would have been alien to her eyes she may have preferred it to the cold calculating stare. She felt like he was already dissecting her on an autopsy table. Fucking xeno creep.

She shivered, turning back to the view-screen, where she enlarged the view of the *Springdawn*. Being chased put one at a tactical disadvantage in the theater of space. At such incredible speeds there was a delay in the picture, they saw the *Springdawn* as it had been seconds before the present, a result of traveling at appreciable fractions of the speed of light. The chasing ship would have more current data, and the range of its weapons and sensors exceeded the range of its optics.

"Conn, sensors, *Springdawn* coming in range of the buoy, showing capacitors charged."

But not firing yet. Shit, were they waiting for a visual? They kept closing the distance.

Unless . . .

Victoria enlarged the view of the *Springdawn*. The enormous ship was rolling clockwise. The dorsal batteries came into view, pivoted towards the *Condor*.

"Huian, full port slip, now! Drop the heat shield and get us to emergency acceleration."

The *Condor* bucked to the left as a wash of active sensor pulses crashed into them. The view screen filled with fire as the *Springdawn's* dorsal batteries discharged, lancing deadly light as bright as any star. The *Condor* shook as if hit by a comet, yawing and rolling from the blast.

"Conn, engineering, starboard ablative wing at six percent. Heat damage to the starboard hull."

Victoria glanced at the damage. "Huian, get us inverted, put the portside wing to them. If they get a direct hit they'll still cut us in half. Time to jump?"

"Three and a half minutes, Ma'am" said Huian. The girl was visibly shaken. At least she knew how much trouble she was in. The Chinese Navy never worried about this sort of shit.

"Huian, you with me?" asked Victoria. Her pilot nodded, still trembling. But her hands were deft on the controls, spinning the *Condor* to point the remaining ablative plating towards the *Springdawn.*

"Carillo," called Victoria over the open microphone, "we've got to keep them away for three minutes, send a swarm down their throat, divide their focus."

"Aye, Vick."

The *Condor* vibrated as a small fleet of live missiles deployed from her tubes, spreading and dashing towards the Dirregaunt ship. They bucked and rocked to avoid point defense systems as they went, deploying flares to confuse sensors. Her rear optics had been completely wiped by the Dirregaunt lasers, but she watched on her tactical view as the *Springdawn's* point defenses started to cut down her missiles, slowing the charging of her main battery's capacitors.

Not enough time, she thought as the number of missiles in the salvo dwindled to single digits. Not a single warhead struck home on the hull of the Dirregaunt battleship.

"Conn, sensors. Showing an explosion on the *Springdawn.*"

Victoria pulled over her sensor screen. "Did one of our warheads make it through?"

"Negative, Vick. Scan suggests it came from inside the *Springdawn.* Spectrum shows traces of exotic matter. The Dirregaunt are reducing their acceleration. Vick, they're breaking off the chase."

It took her a moment to realize the newfound silence was the absence of the marine's warning broadcast, discontinued after the explosion. She rubbed her thumb and index finger over her eyes. Not a recorded broadcast then, Aimes Webb had been aboard the *Springdawn* somehow.

Despite the loss, she bit back a grin. Like hornets in a bee-hive, her marines. The brave little bastard had given his life to give her fair warning. But if he was there, Tessa Baum wouldn't be far behind. The Dirregaunt would have to deal with both before they could safely engage an enemy. In space the Dirregaunt were unstoppable. But well, man to man? Her marines knew how to hurt an enemy, especially one that forgot centuries ago what it meant to be weaker than your enemy.

Victoria sat back against her couch and exhaled. She had fired on the Dirregaunt and lived to tell. They would follow. They had to, she recognized the drive in their captain she saw in herself. Maybe not to the listening post, extracting their coordinates from the busy jump point would take days. But they must know by now that the *Condor* was bound for the Malagath frontier at Kallico'rey, and routes were extremely limited. Somewhere ahead, the *Springdawn* would be waiting. They barely survived this encounter. How would the next play out?

She watched on the forward view screen as the brilliance of Forel gave way to the strange abstract of horizon space, and the familiar chill crept across her skin. Four hours to the listening station was plenty of time to drink herself to sleep. She vacated the captain's couch, passing the First Prince on her way from the conn. A short dip of his head was the only acknowledgement of her victory. Asshole.

CHAPTER 9
LISTENING IN

BEST WISHES WATCHED on his forward view screen as the Paralt carrier broke apart. It was the coward's toll, for peeling away from the hunt so easily. He had watched so many ships burned, blasted, and torn from space that he should no longer feel anything at their passing. But blood coursed through his reserve veins, reddening his vision and twisting his face into a snarl. The pressure built dangerously, but he relished the anger rather than slow his heart. The few fighters who hadn't offered meek, fruitless defense fled deeper into the system. They weren't worth the effort to hunt down.

He knew his rage was misdirected at these poor fools, their vessel jetting plasma into the black scape of Pilum Forel. That he was, in truth, vexed by these space walkers, these *humans* that surprised at every turn. At least one was still aboard, gone to ground as if it knew the ship better than its commander. Two security teams, dead, several communications specialists, including his master hailman, dead. Multiple hull breaches. His primary communications equipment and his superluminal sensors, destroyed. Even that vicious Grah'lhin emissary was dead, though Best Wishes could not bring himself to mourn the passing of the thing. One of their jagged red ships now approached to deliver a new emissary.

The Grah'lhin knew this enemy, one that attacked from within, with skin like blackest sky and anger like the thunder. An enemy that hid between stars, disguising their heat and their place in space and time. Their only tell had been a change in the direction of vented xenon before the trail disappeared. Clue enough to plot their vector. Such primitive engines, and laughable weapons. Pitiful tech from an inconsequential lesser empire. And the cowards survived both attacks while cutting him from within. This was not a familiar fight.

Best Wishes cared little for the pride of his people. The Dirregaunt claimed, collectively, to be the best hunters among the stars. But most had never hunted anything in their lives. They had never known the tedium of waiting in perfect ambush for weeks, striking in a split second incapacitating their prey with a singular blow. Best Wishes was the best hunter in the galaxy, not because he was Dirregaunt, but because he was Best Wishes. *Then came the spacewalker.* Colorless, odorless. How could one hunt a devil? By loosing another devil who could.

His first officer approached him. "Sir, one of the Grah'lhin vessels has docked."

Best Wishes turned. "Well, let us meet the lesser devil. Come, Modest Bearing," he said. A security team escorted them from the bridge. There would be escorts everywhere, he knew, until the second spacewalker could be found and expunged. A troublesome burden, the coddling grated his nerves the entire way to the shuttle bay. Security made everything sluggish.

The Grah'lhin ship was a mass of hardened edges and uncomfortable crystalline protrusions barely larger than a shuttle. It was a dull red, the hull slightly translucent, though not enough to reveal what lay within. An iris air-lock twisted open on the underside of the cutter. Three Grah'lhin skittered out of the hatch, and down one of the legs upon which the ship rested. The sight of them still tickled the primal part of his brain, telling him to run. They approached Best Wishes, a mass of clicking legs and mandibles.

Weapons were raised by the security team, but Best Wishes held them off with a curt gesture. He had seen one of the creatures angry now, and knew what he saw barely qualified as awake for these xenos. Besides, the personal lasers might not stop the Graylings should they choose to attack. The Grah'lhin still wanted Victoria. The lead Grah'lhin stooped slightly to meet Best Wishes' eyes, the protective layers sliding back from the moist sensory band in exactly the same fashion as his predecessor.

"*The humans aboard your ship, I will hunt them.*"

Best Wishes glanced to his security officer, who offered confused eyes. How had the creature known there were space walkers aboard? The previous emissary had not been granted access to communications, nor ever asked to use them before it died. Best Wishes was missing something here. But more important matters were at stake.

"You can find it?"

Several sets of vestigial wings buzzed underneath thick carapace. "*Perhaps, Dirregaunt Commander. Did I not tell you of their cunning? Of their . . . malice? Few prey are more dangerous. And Victoria has escaped you.*"

"You also told me they walk in the void, and hide between stars. I now know I did not lend due worth to your words. Now among my crew rest the dead of the hunt, in storage until we can take them home."

More mandibles clicked before the Grah'lhin answered.

"*They practice the highest of subterfuge. Fall not to legend, Dirregaunt Commander, neither ignore the data your senses present you. Trust my experience, and open your ship to me that I might find them.*"

"Commander," interrupted Modest Bearing, "You can't mean to let these monstrosities loose on the ship? We're adding to one malicious infestation with another."

A looked quelled his first officer. Now was not the time for half-measures, not when the space walkers forced the *Springdawn* to retreat while victory was close. Not when they had ruptured the hull and sent his on-duty sensor and communications teams spiraling into the void. He turned back to the insectoid aliens and their uncomfortable ship.

"Go. Find me the humans that remain on my vessel."

Victoria waited impatiently as the magnetic seals secured the *Condor* to the docking port of the listening post. She began to climb the ladder to the dorsal hatch as soon as the air pressure began to equalize, and by the time she reached the top rungs the hatch was being pulled open to reveal a wide toothy grin.

"Vick, you ol' starhound, get on up here."

"Jax," she said as she took his hand, black and gnarled as aged rosewood. As she climbed out of the hatch he pulled her into a fierce hug. She was greeted to a close-up of his graying crew cut as he laughed and slapped her on the back.

"Yeah, yeah, I get it, you ain't seen a woman in years," she said as she extricated herself from his grip. Red emerged from the hatch behind her and offered his hand.

"Good to see you, Jax."

Jax took his hand, that grin never leaving his face.

Somehow the man never failed to lift Victoria up just that little bit. His bearing was infectious.

"What's this I hear about you having some presents for ol' Jax and his merry men?"

"You can marry men on your own time, captain. What do you know?" asked Victoria.

Jax laughed. "Well, I know you two are making trails. The net is all afire, and word with the Jenursa is that a Dirregaunt dreadnought is lookin' for a little ship fits the *Condor*'s likeness. Amazing how gabby we all get when the Big Three are in the neighborhood. We got told to head here. FTL con is lit up, needs both our inputs. Weren't sure what we'd find here, but your bird looks beat to all hell."

"Those 'Gaunt batteries are no joke. Tagged us near three hundred K-K."

Jax whistled. "That's a damn sight further than we thought. New generation?"

"Some high-profile task force prick, gets all the shiny new toys."

"And just how did you come on the scope of this specialist? Let me guess, you spent five minutes talking to him and he declared humanity enemies of the Praetory."

Victoria rolled her eyes, then twisted and called down the hatch. "Hey F.P., come on up."

It was her turn to grin as the First Prince ascended the ladder. Slowly, the Malagath emerged from the hatch, followed by his retinue. The otherwise immutable smile slid from Jax's face as he looked up into the blue hued face of First Prince Tavram.

"Vick, girl, oh what have you got the Vultures mixed up in now?"

"Just a millennia long war between two galactic supergiants. Oh, did I mention that this is First Prince Tavram?

Anyway, I'd better get at that message terminal. First Prince, your crew is free to move about the station and stretch out. I know they're a bit cramped aboard the *Condor*. We should be safe here, Bargult doesn't know about this listening post."

"Bargult?" asked Jax, "How does that overgrown lady-bug weigh into it?"

"You're not gonna believe this, Jax, but I've got marines aboard the Dirregaunt cruiser. One of them sent a databurst we unpacked in Horizon. More intel on the Dirregaunt than we've ever seen. Equipment, engine frequencies, deck plans, you name it," said Victoria, heading for the communication center with Red in tow. Jax skipped to catch up.

"Hold on Vick, back it up. You have *marines* on a *Dirregaunt* ship."

"Boarded at Taru station, along with our mutual friend. Bug bastard is helping them find me. Goddamn bastard knows we're headed for the Malagath front."

They passed members of Jax's crew already taking advantage of the short break afforded by the automated space station's relative luxury. She couldn't help slowing her pace slightly as the two shirtless marines jogged past on the track that went around the outer ring of the station. Exercise bikes were well and good, but a body needed to stretch its legs from time to time, see just how far it could be pushed and keep running.

Her own crew would be pulling maintenance in shifts, replacing what hurt they could and patching what they couldn't. She passed a porthole, through which the stubby black nose of the *Condor* was silhouetted against the bright blue star of the local system. Crewmembers could already be seen in vacuum suits outside the ship, seeing to the external damage the near miss of the *Springdawn's* weapons had caused. She shivered despite the heat of the station, remembering the way the Dirregaunt commander had cut apart the *Dreadstar* after she picked up the First Prince. He must be sharp as a razor to have tracked her this far. What might such a commander have done to earn his position?

"You cold, Vick?" asked Red.

Victoria shook her head, taking one final look at the lifeless planetoid around which the station orbited and moving away from the window. She ducked under some piping to reach the hatch to the communication node. She heaved it open, with Red's help and Jax's supervision. The latch clicked into its bracket and Victoria looked at her counterpart.

"Age before beauty," he said as he swung onto the ladder. His grin was the last thing to disappear down the access. Red followed, and by the time Victoria was sliding down the ladder Jax had already began booting up the faster-than-light communications terminal. Her retinal implants interfaced with the station's computers, briefly displaying notifications of unread messages in her Union Earth account before returning to standby. The number had slowly rose as she ignored more and more of it, and now reached the low thousands. She figured if it were worth reading, it would have come through an FTL crypto.

The terminal looked like so much junk to her, framed by twisted snakes of segmented metal wires tunneling every which-way into the walls, ceiling and the floor, where the crypto array hung beneath the station. An ancient display and old-fashioned mechanical keyboard were the only visible interface to one of the most advanced devices the human race had ever concocted. Even if most of the improved technology was stolen, they had worked out the initial process themselves. A layer of fine dust coated both, which she brushed off as she took Jax's place on the bolted stool.

It took only a few moments to input her captain's credentials, Jax rested a hand on her shoulder as he leaned forward to read the message from the Secretary of State and Colony with her. She felt him tense up as he scanned the words of the FTL crypto.

"Aw shit," said Victoria, slamming her fist on the keyboard and turning from the display. Little fiberglass keys sprung loose from the device. "Fucking shit, fuck. No fucking way, I won't believe Wong sent that fucking message. She wants us to hand over the First Prince? Are you fucking kidding me?"

"It's black and white, Vick," said Jax. He didn't look pleased about it either, it broke every tenet the privateers operated by. Situations involving ferrying the Big Three were never well established by State and Colony, but surrendering rescues to their attackers was tantamount to bounty hunting. A high profile turnover like this could break humanity's tenuous reputation in the Orion Spur.

"Goddammit. What do you think the Malagath are going to do when they find out we have orders to hand them over to the Dirregaunt? We'd have to kill them ourselves, and the crew would never stand for it."

"Ain't got a choice, girl. Can't disregard an order from S&C, no matter who your rescue is."

"There's always a choice, Jax. Red? What do you think?"

Major Calhoun had, up until this point, remained quiet as he digested the unsavory message. He shrugged, weariness creeping into his voice. "My marines will keep order if it comes to that. But it can't come to that, it'd break the *Condor*. And a broken ship is a dead ship out this far from Earth."

"Great, so break every rule in the book, betray a very

powerful member of the Malagath ruling class we swore to protect, and stem a mutiny aboard the *Condor* when they find out we're to hand over the xenos they taught to play poker. When you put it like that it sounds so simple."

"I never told you command would be easy, Vick," Jax said, "In the meantime, let's see about getting that tech offloaded. We're due to meet the *Sagan* in a couple days, we'll hand off to them. I'll crypto that databurst back to the U.E. while we're at it. You make it back; you'll all be heroes."

"Traitorous, backstabbing heroes. You can take the tech. We'll take the *Springdawn*. But you gotta do something for me. I'm going to need every bag of tricks you got handy, starting with your gravitic buoy. Seems we lost ours"

"Anything you need, Vick. However we can help."

Tessa had been a marine for 12 years, three of those in space. She was a veteran of countless hostile encounters, domestic and xeno, where she proved her iron nerves and steel resolve through strength of arms and will alike. She'd seen battle brothers fall, some who would survive and some who would never rise again. She always kept fighting. When she felt that second explosion translate through the hull of the *Springdawn*, when Aimes' broadcast cut off so suddenly, she knew he was dead. She ran. She found a secluded corner of the massive ship, climbed up a tree, and bawled until she passed out from sheer exhaustion.

Now her suit's alarm woke her, warning her of approaching footfalls. Cautiously, she peeked beneath the false canopy, and immediately retreated out of line-of-sight. A Grayling passed beneath her refuge, lumbering on patrol with a retinue of Dirregaunt security forces and their handheld lasers.

She didn't like the implication of an alliance between the two, however temporary it might be. Humanity had crossed paths with Bargult on more than one occasion and become something of an interest to the Grayling, and he could, unfortunately, provide the *Springdawn* with a good deal of accurate intel regarding the habits of the privateers.

Plus, she didn't like her odds against even a few of the beasts. The first had caught her by surprise, and she gambled away far too much of her dwindling ammunition to break the Dirregaunt barricade and escape the berserk xeno. One of the Dirregaunt had tagged her with a laser as she'd left, slagging most of the ablative material on her leg. It still wasn't clear how the Grayling nervous system interpreted the data viewed through their sensory band, but she doubted the foliage she had stuck to her vacuum suit would do much good.

"Well girl, you knew this would be a one-way ticket as soon as you stepped on board," she said. They hadn't seen the last of the *Condor*, either. Tessa had to be ready if she were to offer them any aid, and that meant learning the extent to which the *Springdawn* was tracking the Vultures.

She pulled up her incomplete schematics of the *Springdawn*, trying to ignore the curling pain in her stomach. It had been almost a day since she had eaten, and nothing burned calories like combat. The vacuum suit was near perfect at collecting sweat, urine, and exhaled moisture to return to the body, and as long as her algae cultures held up she had all the oxygen she could breath. The protein shots she had held off until she direly needed them. The emergency sustenance would do nothing to cure her aching belly, however.

On her schematic she had a pretty good idea of where the a few major stations were, but no clue where the most important compartment in the ship was. The bridge was still a mystery. The Dirregaunt used messengers to communicate most orders and information. One of them might have information she could use to help the *Condor*. She had been tracking the paths they took; it had been useful to learn the fastest routes through the sprawling ship. And her weapon just so happened to have the perfect attachment for waylaying one, if she could avoid the patrols. It would be dangerous. If she were caught doing it, the Dirregaunt and Graylings could flush her out and expose her.

Her best chance would be in the area she'd dubbed 'The Boonies', on account of the rough scrub and foliage. A foggy path cut through the compartment, funneling would-be messengers and their security details down a predictable path. On Earth, no military would be that sloppy when enemy agents were running around. But this wasn't Earth, and the Dirregaunt had long forgotten what it meant to be the hunted. She began the slow process of charging the cryo-round. She had to be perfect, very little of the sedative remained, and she couldn't afford to make a lot of noise. Slowly, she worked her way into the foliage above and waited for the next patrol.

Aesop watched the sun set over the lifeless planetoid beneath the listening post as he hung, inverted, outside the aft portside wing. A misnomer, as no airfoil existed on the *Condor*. Really, it was only a sloped bulwark of ablative plating and electromagnetic armor designed to give the *Condor* a fighting chance against the advanced weaponry of a universe that made her look like a biplane in a world of jet engines. The lasers employed by blue-navy warships on Earth could cut metal at almost a hundred kilometers, but some xenotech variants could sheer a starliner in half at a thousand times that range. Those warships he left behind long ago on a planet that might never move on from its quarrelsome ways.

He never tired of the microgravity of orbit, caught in a constant free-fall above the black surface of the alien planetoid as a shroud of stars revealed themselves in the night. He felt completely at home. On Earth he'd always felt out of place. He had laid on the sand after the invasion of Tehran, staring up at the stars and the black smoke rising over the city, unable to reconcile how little the discovery of life in the universe had diminished humanity's need to slaughter each other over such petty things. Transgressions older than the written word were brought to bear while ships jumped between stars, trading and making contact with dozens of other civilizations.

Two years after the fall of Iran, Aesop left the Israeli Special Forces and began studying engineering and xenotechnology in London, in hopes of enlisting in the Union Earth Navy and seeing the stars. The privateer corps noticed him first, and he found himself aboard the *U.E.P. Blacksail,* learning that the greater expanse was not so different from the rat race down on Earth. Instead of America, China, and India, it was the Malagath Empire, the Kossovoldt, and the Dirregaunt Praetory shaping the local galactic theater while the rest scrabbled for what the Big Three could not be bothered with. Sometimes peacefully, sometimes with a knife at the throat.

And yet, as he clamped down the tiny sensor nodule, it was not all bad. Altruism and idealism existed in the universe, albeit as the exception. The Thorivult allowed human cohabitation on their developed worlds, for no other reason than a shared need of oxygenated atmosphere. The

Jenursa had seen the families repaired by the privateer's refugee initiative, and offered full safe passage through their territory and a support network to the Privateers, so long as their mission remained unchanged.

Aesop's radio clicked in his ear, bringing him back from his thoughts. Aurea had remained onboard the *Condor* to assist with the repairs.

"The node is interfacing, Human Aesop. My screen shows full integration with all two-hundred and thirty-one sensors installed, with five still nonfunctional," she said. His retinal implants confirmed the report, but it was always nice to work with a partner, and the Malagath engineer had proven as congenial as she was brilliant. He would miss her when they reached Kallico'Rey

"That close call baked us pretty good, what did the First Prince have to say about it?"

"The Prince does not discuss matters of strategy with such as I. But I felt he was impressed with your captain's actions. She has a mind like the enemy, it has allowed her to survive him, despite these primitive means."

"That's my *Condor* you're talking about, Aurea. Even if you have made her your pet project until we get you back home. Sometimes I think you'd marry the GSD if you could."

"Human Aesop!" said Aurea, sounding scandalized, "The Malagath do not marry inanimate pieces of technology! I simply see additional . . . applications . . . for your primitive technology that you have not considered."

"Oh? Those applications being?" he asked.

A lilting chirp flowed through the radio, not unlike morning birdsong. The female equated form of their laughter. The male version sounded somewhere between a frog's croak and a bull's trumpet. "You will see, Human Aesop," she said. Her tinkering had already net several improvements, albeit at the cost of an increased electrical demand. They devised a workaround for the GSD breaker box to accommodate the extra voltage. He had no idea how she was doing it with no knowledge of circuitry. In fact, she tended to ignore most of the computerized aspect of their equipment, dismissing the green silicon boards as junk while she made fundamental changes in line with Malagath design philosophies. Even his chief engineer was humbled by her results.

He sighed, maneuvering the skiff to the next damaged sensor node to be replaced. A soft green corona had begun to appear over the polar regions of the planetoid. "Are you sure you wouldn't rather be out here with me than cooped up on the ship?"

"Once in the void was quite enough, Human Aesop!"

Victoria woke suddenly and fully. No period of fatigue, no instant of transitory confusion. Dreamless sleep was replaced by a softly blinking light on the atmospheric monitoring panel in her quarters, and the soft snores of the marine next to her, one of the *Huxley*'s. Even having not slept since before the Malagath refugees were taken off the *Dreadstar*, it took copious amounts of whiskey and the substantial efforts of the marine to finally exhaust her to the point of sleep. Her retinal implants winked on, showing six hours had passed by, no alarm for another two. And yet she knew that sleep would not return, only the insistent demand for attention from the blinking panel. She hated that damned light.

She attempted to slide out of her rack, swearing softly as she accidentally planted an elbow in the stomach of the marine, *James? Jayce? J-something,* as she crawled across him. A painful grunt was her only answer, but he simply rolled over and resumed snoring. His fault for being in the way, she decided as she noiselessly pulled on her uniform with the practiced motions that had aided many stealthy escapes over the years.

She thumbed the door panel, making her way aft through the eerily quiet ship and towards the connection ring that married the *Condor* to the Pilum Forel listening post. The soft orchestra of the privateer ship lulled as she climbed the ladder. First, the sounds of the artificial gravity generator faded. Then the electric bus, then finally the motor generators. It was all replaced by the hum of the station's ventilation and the buzzing of the fluorescent lights. The station smelled of dust. It was sometimes months between privateer and resupply visits, and the station was otherwise unmanned to conserve resources.

There were seven such stations scattered across the Orion Spur, hidden away in otherwise unremarkable systems where caution and subterfuge might keep them secret. Three more were being constructed from prefabricated modules, to be placed as close as possible to the Kossovoldt front towards the galactic core, on the other side of the human's current reach. Humanity's ever expanding dominion over the stars had been her life's work. God, if they just weren't so hopelessly outgunned at every turn she might actually get somewhere.

Victoria finally found herself in the observation ring at the top of the station, not even knowing it had been her destination. She leaned forward against the composite window and watched showers of sparks fly from vacuum-suited welders making repairs to the *Condor*. The ship itself she could barely make out, a slightly darker patch on the perfect midnight black of the planetoid below. Only the silhouette of the hot-work defined her ship's narrow profile.

The hatch to the observation deck slid open, and Victoria turned to see First Prince Tavram stooping to fit through the entrance. She turned back to the *Condor,* allowing him a moment to compose himself before joining her.

"I greet you, Human Victoria," he said in a passable English. He nodded slightly in answer to her questioning stare. "Your station is equipped with a small library. Within I discovered a Kossovoldt-Human dictionary, and some small history volumes."

"Shit, I probably should have blocked your access to those. We're not used to hosting xenos at the listening posts. I suppose most history books are short compared to yours," she replied. Victoria paused. "You learned English in six hours?"

"But of course. Is that not the purpose of the dictionary?"

She shook her head, realizing only after that the subtleties of the gesture were probably lost on him. Speaking English with a xeno seemed to have disarmed her somewhat.

"Captain, the degree to which your people have wounded each other is both astounding and terrifying. It seems your home planet does not need the lesser empires; it is constantly at war with itself. Do you know that few, if any, cultures survive to colonize after turning the power of atomic weapons upon themselves? When you first told me of this I will admit I did not believe you, just as I did not believe in beings that walk in the void."

"War is a habit we just can't kick. We're trying to do better. We've got unified colonies, a non-nationalistic government under no currency and no dominant local earth language."

"And the privateers, extending a hand to starfarers

caught in most dire straits."

"Mixed bag, that. It seems like every friend we make; we end up with twice as many enemies. How many more are we going to have before Earth is ready to step out of the shadows?"

She turned back to the *Condor*. The First Prince remained with her, his back reflected in the polymer window as he gazed out the other side of the ring towards the expanse of stars.

"One more, at least, Captain Victoria. *He* is out there. Waiting? A certainty. He will not stop until he knows I am dead. It is why he was chosen, despite his low birth."

"Low birth?" asked Victoria.

"Best Wishes is of the servant's caste, believed unfit to hold position or command even a shuttle, let alone a strength battle group. His success is worrisome to many, and more still hope for his failure."

"Shit, if he were from Earth we'd have made a movie about him. A real feel-good underdog popcorn flick." Victoria paused. "I guess the fucker has a lot riding on this."

The First Prince nodded. She wondered if he'd picked up the gesture from her crew or from his reading. Just that simple bob twisted her guts, knowing she was to condemn him to death or worse at the hands of the Dirregaunt. Her hands sweat on the rail as she watched the corona blossom into a full, green borealis around the planet's poles. She couldn't stab him in the back like that. Not without looking him in the eye while she did it.

"Prince Tavram, my government has ordered me to hand you over to the Praetory," she said.

The First Prince's reflection stilled as his breath caught, then resumed. "I thought as much, Captain Victoria. Human Red was recalcitrant after the parley with Captain

Jackson, I knew it to be ill portent. May I ask why they have decided to do so?"

"It's not so tough to puzzle out. War means the humans advance. Taking you home means less salvage, less stolen tech, less progress and more risk as humanity slips further behind the competition."

The first prince was silent for a time.

"Captain Victoria, would you die for the Vultures?"

"Come again?"

"After we escaped from Best Wishes, my crew witnessed several injured engineers returning to the engine room despite the danger, many sustaining further bodily harm. I did not understand why they subjected themselves to such risk instead of tending to their own needs. Examining your literature illuminated a trend of those who put others before themselves. Among the Malagath, a captain is expected to put himself before his crew. The value of a skilled commander outweighs any number of the peasantry. Would you do the same, were you weighed against the sum of your Vultures? Or would you do as your soldier did at Forel?"

Victoria stood a moment before answering. "Any of those history books of yours mention a place called Chernobyl?"

The First Prince joined her at the rail, admiring the Aurora. "An electrical facility, the power of the atom escaped your people and caused severe damage in the place called Chernobyl. Radioactive particles contaminated the local ecosystem."

Victoria nodded, now sure the First Prince would understand its meaning. "Ten days after the accident, the disaster crews discovered irradiated water pooling beneath the reactor. Left alone, the fuel would have burned its way down and caused a steam explosion that could have killed millions."

"Obviously this did not occur, else the shape of your history would be very different. How did they stop it?"

"Someone figured out the only way to drain it was a valve at the bottom of the pool. Three men volunteered to swim in irradiated water to open it. They knew it was a one-way trip. They never hesitated. They swam down to that valve with nothing but a broken lamp, and they opened that fucking valve, and they stopped one of the biggest potential disaster's in Earth's history. All three of them died."

"All three sacrificed themselves instead of retreating to safety?"

"Sacrifice is who we are. It defines us as human. We take bullets for each other, jump on grenades, lay down on the wire. You want to know if I'd die for my crew? Aw hell. I'd like to think I wouldn't. I'd like to think my rational mind would stop me, shake me, ask me what the fuck I'm doing. But I know the score. The answer is yes, and I'd be kicking myself all the way down to hell."

First Prince Tavram clasped his hands behind his back and stepped to the opposite side of the observation ring. "Join me, if you would, Captain Victoria."

Tentatively, she approached the tall, slender figure.

"My home system lies in this direction," he said, indicating a quadrant of the sky. "It lays just inward of the leading edge of our galactic blade. We are close enough that several of our constellations can be discerned, named for great Malagath war vessels destroyed by the Dirregaunt and the Kossovoldt in this endless war I sought to at least forestall. Many, many starfarers died to bring me this far, as was my right as their captain and their First Prince to spend their lives like currency. It is the way of the Malagath, and I have not known another until now. Perhaps the Malagath insulate themselves from the lesser empires to their detriment. Or perhaps your people's altruism affects me to mine."

The First Prince turned to Victoria. "In accordance with the orders of your government, I will turn myself over to Best Wishes, willingly, on the condition that you continue your course to take the survivors of my crew to the Malagath frontier. I will lay down on your grenade if you take the last of my starfarers home to finish my work."

CHAPTER 10
UNTO THE DARK

"THIS ISN'T RIGHT, GIRL. Ain't no one would think less of you tossing on those orders."

Victoria could count on one hand the number of times she'd seen Jax in a rage. His crew was daisy-chaining the last of the Malagath tech from the *Condor* to the *Huxley*.

"It's a good deal, Jax. The First Prince for the *Condor* and the crew of the *Dreadstar*. If that Dirregaunt Commander will make a deal, that is," said Victoria.

"Yeah, well you better hope he hasn't made a white whale out of you."

"Just cause I can't keep my figure as I get old don't give you leave to be an asshole," teased Victoria. Jax didn't laugh.

"I may be the asshole, but that crypto smells like grade-A horseshit. We're handing this junk off to the *Chesapeake* and then maybe we can come back and find you. Assuming there's anything left . . ."

Victoria gave him one final hug, then slid down the ladder while he sealed the airlock above her. The warm noises of the *Condor* welcomed her, and she made her way to the conn with only the buzz of the engines for company. Hui-an and Tavram were there as she arrived, the First Prince moving aside that she might take her command couch.

"Huian, cast off. Take us round the southern pole and accelerate to point-two."

"Aye Skipper,"

The sounds of the engine increased as the *Condor* pulled away from the listening post. The view rotated as Victoria's pilot accelerated through the orbit of the planetoid and brought the star into view. The horizon jump would take six hours.

"Somewhere on the other side of the star, death left the light on for us. Let's not keep him up too late."

Beneath Tessa, three Dirregaunt sailors padded softly through the path. The messenger was obvious by his sense of urgency and flanked by two armed sentries, but no Grayling. Best odds she'd seen all day, which was good because the battery on the tranquilizer unit was running low, even staggering the refrigeration unit to keep the round ready. She had no way to charge it once it was dead. It was now or never. She sighted the messenger on her optics, switching the unit back into charge mode.

One of the security team stopped. "Did you hear that?" he asked? Tessa cursed. The sedative attachment had a tell-tale whisper of a whine, so low her suit could barely pick it up. The other two perked up, ears swiveling to listen for her telltales. No choice, she was made. She stilled her breath and fired, causing the messenger to jump.

"Something bit me!" he shouted. Lasers were raised.

"The space walker is here."

"Where?"

"Ahead, in the trees to the left of the path. Cook it on my mark"

Shit! Dirregaunt hearing. She jumped down from the

tree just as it exploded, landing badly and rolling into the thick foliage. The lasers cut off, and her vibration sensors told her something was on the move towards her.

"Not going for help," she murmured, "Time to see who the best hunters in the galaxy are."

She caught side of a stalk swaying to her right 2 o'clock. Damn but these bastards were fast. From where she lay she could still see the messenger, standing idly haven taken two or three steps towards the way he'd come. She had to move, *now.*

She slid her combat knife out of its sheath as quietly as she could, but cursed when the vibration sensors stilled for an instant. They didn't have a scent, but they sure as hell had her sound. Well, she might be able to do something about that. Being quiet had failed, maybe it was time to try being loud. Dirregaunt ears would close to protect them against loud noises. She held her rifle above her head and fired a single round, then dashed towards what she hoped was the Dirregaunt security detail. Time was even more a premium now, her rifle would travel a long way in this ship, and there were Graylings to worry about.

She came upon him before she'd expected to, and from his startled posture, he hadn't expected her to go on the offensive. There was a moment's hesitation in his eyes as he took in her black face mask, enough hesitation for her to put a gloved fist into his midsection. An armored knee followed it, and a stomp to what would have been his solar plexus once the security officer hit the ground. Before she could finish the job a weight hit her from behind, bowling her over onto the soft deck of the ship. The wind was knocked from her, and a claw twisted around her arm and flipped Tessa's belly upwards.

Claws raked against the composite plating of her chest

piece, and a mouth full of tiny, sharp teeth snapped at her throat as she got a hand around one of two bony protrusions on the Dirregaunt's chest. The xeno was larger, but not heavier, and she was able to keep his jaws away from her even as the Dirregaunt's claws probed for a weak spot. It found one, on her side, punching through a layer of Kevlar to puncture the suit's inner wall. Her suit's computer blared alarms as it self-sealed, but she could feel where the claw scored across her hip. *Time to return the favor.*

She angled her knife up and jammed it into the Dirregaunt's side, pushing him off as he spasmed. She kicked her way to her feet, hand against her side. She wasn't equipped to self-medicate, and between the pain causing stinging tears the threat of blood loss she hoped the scratch wasn't deep enough to need stitches. Christ, it felt like he'd hit bone.

She stumbled back to the path, grabbing the sedated messenger and hauling ass through the outboard foliage. If she could reach the secondary stores, she could be reasonably sure that no one could interrupt her. She stopped briefly, smearing dirt over the blood that had splashed her suit. Any kind of foreign biological scent the Dirregaunt could track, and the shot had brought company. Tessa could make out the backs of the Graylings as they pushed through foliage, heedless of noise or trail. She laughed inside her suit. They were making more than enough noise to cover her escape. Damn that hip wound hurt.

By the time the sedative wore off several hours later, Tessa had started developing the early signs of a fever. Whatever alien microbes the Dirregaunt's claws carried took hold in her body, storming the walls of her immune system with an infection it had no idea how to fight. The response was to raise her temperature, try to cook out the intruder. It would be the correct biological response for an Earth infection, but Dirregaunt basal body temperatures were significantly higher, especially when those big brains of theirs were working.

Tessa slapped the courier as he started to come out of his fugue.

"Wake up," she demanded, "I don't have all day."

The Dirregaunt shook himself, blinking away the effects of the tranquilizer, then panicking as he realized his wrists had been bound to a storage rack by the vines that snaked around the locker. She slapped him again. He finally took in his full situation. She must look a sight, all slathered in leaves and dirt and Dirregaunt blood.

"Please," he stammered, shying away from her open palm. It was good that he cowed easy, she was starting to get dizzy. Might have missed the third swing.

"Tell me your name."

"I-I am Earthen Musk, space walker. I am a runner only; I have nothing of value to you."

"You carried a message, from who to where? Out with it."

"F-From the Commander to secondary security. He is ordering them to allow the Grah'lhin to hunt for you unescorted."

"You came from the bridge?"

"Yes, but I am just a runner. I don't want to hunt your people, none of us do, none except Best Wishes."

Tessa paused. "There is dissent among the crew?"

"The Commander is a low-born mad dog, his obsession is getting us killed, we are within a space tear of the Malagath Empire."

Disloyal little chickenshit. Tessa wasn't precisely fond of thinking that put some folks inherently above others. It certainly colored her opinion of her captive.

"There are others feel the same way?"

The captured courier fluttered his ears, the Dirregaunt affirmative. *A broken ship is a dead ship.* Something the major always said. A conflict like that could throw the *Springdawn* into chaos. It just needed the right catalyst.

"What would happen if your commander was . . . out of the picture?"

Earthen musk snarled. "The first officer would take us home. Our mission is over, we destroyed the *Dreadstar*. There is nothing to be gained by chasing lesser empire rats through the airlocks." He became more animate as the sedative continued to wear off. He paused. "You don't know where the bridge is, do you?"

Tessa leaned against her rifle to keep from falling over. "No," she admitted.

The Dirregaunt courier considered for a moment. "If I tell you how to find it, will you let me go? You will know the commander, there are red stripes in his mane, and the left side of his face is scarred."

She couldn't let him live, not a chance. Not when he might wriggle out and warn someone. She had killed the courier as soon as he trod the path where she'd waited for him.

"Of course," she said.

"I cannot hear your heartbeat through that armor, if even you have one. I cannot smell your fear. I cannot tell if you are lying to me, space walker."

She leaned in close. His feet scrabbled against the decking trying to squeeze every inch he could away from her black composite helmet. "Where is the bridge?"

After he told her she killed him quickly. Tessa stood, leaning for a moment against the rack of what might have been antibiotics, for all she knew. Didn't matter if they were, she figured. They'd be as like to kill her as cure her, if her body could metabolize them at all. She shouldered her rifle and started making her way towards the bridge of the vast star ship.

———

For the third time, Best Wishes found himself clicking his claws against his chest bones. He stilled his hands, and attempted to still his mind. He could not, his heart quickened whenever he thought of this minor captain, this *Victoria*. The *Condor* was on its way, the superluminal sensor signature matched that obtained at Pilum. The imprecise lesser empire engines had forced them out of interstellar travel outside the orbit of the first two planets in this system. She would have to pass him to draw close enough to the star's gravity to pierce space again.

Though his ship held a mere half-million kilometers from the first planet, he could not see it through the cloud of thick, ionized gasses that swirled along this star's orbital plane. Despite the effect the gas had displayed among his crew it was proper to hunt here, unseen in the brilliant miasmic disc that stretched across the inner three planets. The light filtering through the cloud had caused hallucinations to several of his starfarers who had viewed it through the infrared spectrum granted by their top eye, and most had closed it out of recourse. His remained open, he would brook no such handicap on this hunt. The stunning infrareds played within the cloud, shifting and swirling hypnotically on the view screen. He could almost see patterns in the haze.

Behind him, another of the Grah'lhin haunted the observation ring, precisely as his predecessor had. No, that was a poor way to call it. He was beginning to understand that each creature was not an individual in the truest sense, but he couldn't yet determine the full extent of their connection.

The creature noticed his regard, and leaned over the rail, lowering its sensory band to receive his address.

"How fares the search for the additional humans?"

"There is but one, Dirregaunt Commander. But you are unfortunate, it is one of the warriors that infests your battleship. It is not easily found in your infernal jungles."

"How can that be?" asked Best Wishes. The damned thing should be leaving a trail through the ship wherever it went.

"I am uncertain. We have never encountered them in such an environment. It appears . . . experienced in such, and is offered a multitude of ground in which to conceal itself. The Grah'lhin have no such places on our worlds."

Best Wishes had no desire to imagine what hellscape spawned the Grah'lhin, so he spun instead to his first officer. Modest Bearing had been regarding him with a rarely seen look, which he scrubbed from his face as Best Wishes turned to him. *He is beginning to doubt my orders.* That was what the split-second of honesty told him. How many others offered similar judgments to his command? Modest Bearing was among his most loyal officers. From the shamed expression he could tell his first officer had tracked his line of thought. His own face must seem rather dark.

"What say you on this matter?" he demanded.

Modest Bearing shifted uncomfortably. "We hear the creature not often over the noise of the *Springdawn*. It has no odor and no heat. If it is true that this people still has a warrior caste, then it is a fearsome foe indeed. Two more of the Grah'lhin have fallen, though it seems content to ignore our security teams. Perhaps it knows the Grah'lhin have a better chance of finding it."

"What would your course of action be?"

"It is not my place to say, Commander."

Best Wishes chopped the protest with a wave of his hand. His first officer cleared his throat. "We lay in wait on the very cusp of Imperium space. How long until word reaches the Malagath of our presence? Their restitution will not be gentle, and every moment these humans delay us is greater danger in which we find ourselves. Dozens have been lost already."

Best Wishes' eyes flicked momentarily to the sensor station, where Dutiful Heiress maintained the watch. Modest Bearing followed his gaze.

"Fortunate, Commander, that she was not at the forward array during the breach. The creature cannot hide forever; you will have vengeance."

"You overstep, Modest. My duty is to the Praetory and the hunt, not my flawed and fruitless lusts. The losses at the communication hub and the forward sensor array have reminded me where my focus need be."

"Your mission was to destroy the *Dreadstar,* and you have done that. Is it even the First Prince that you chase still? Or this lesser empire captain who bested you?"

Best Wishes unfurled the claws he had been digging into the pads on his palms, examining the tiny pricks of blood. His first officer's arguments had merit. A wise commander might heed the words of his crew and withdraw. But a bold commander would not, and how could Best Wishes face the Praetory having come this far only to give up? Modest Bearing could not understand the weight on his back.

"Commander," called Dutiful Heiress, "the *Condor* is

here, just outside the orbit of the third planet."

"On the screen," he barked in reply. The sensor data appeared on the forward view bank, a small spike in the quantum turbulence that indicated a primitive ship slipping back into the primary universe. It was a match to the one analyzed in Pilum Forel. Instants later the gravitic distortion vanished, as if it had never been there at all. A moment later it was back, but he wondered if it was really the *Condor*. *The humans are as ghosts.*

Only fitting that the Dirregaunt should hunt the ethereal.

———

"Tac, let 'em fly, rails and relays," said Victoria. The *Condor* shuddered and protested as no less than a dozen small missiles rushed away from the ship in as many vectors. A final *ka-chunk* signaled the mechanical linkage of the *Huxley's* gravitic buoy detaching from the belly of the privateer ship, ready to impersonate the *Condor's* gravitic signature. The newly improved Gravitic Stealth Device was powered up, a godsend even if Yuri couldn't make heads or tails of what that Malagath engineer had done to it.

"Conn, tactical. The comm relays are away, standard spread. But you can bet he'll track 'em to the source quick. Dobermans show laser links holding steady, but this gas is cutting the range down. They'll be ready to bite when you call."

"Good. Huian, get some distance and then broadcast the invitation. Point-two towards the star. He's out there somewhere."

The *Condor* rattled as her engines accelerated the ship towards the interior of the star system.

"Avery, any sign of the *Springdawn* yet?"

"Negative Vick, this cloud is killing our passives. Let's hope he's as blind as we are."

"We'll see him soon enough. Huian, open the link."

The *Condor's* tight-beam communication synced with the gravitic buoy, which then broadcasted a similarly narrow swath of data through six remote communication relays that Victoria had launched upon entering the system. The relays were patterned to have the most distance possible between each device in the sequence, but the signal attenuation was worth the added security. The array was meant to buy time, as the *Springdawn* would have to detect, maneuver to, and intercept each relay to find the gravitic buoy, and eventually the *Condor*.

"Knock, knock," said Victoria as the sixth and final relay picked up the signal and began to broadcast a wide message, an invitation for the Dirregaunt commander to open a video link between the ships. Victoria was using a Dirregaunt communication protocol. Most species became unsettled when you spoke to them in their own language with their own technology, but would it have the same effect on the Big Three?

"Conn sensors, superluminal contact. The *Springdawn* is at the first relay."

"Piggyback the message for Baum, hopefully she's still alive over there," said Victoria.

A positive status appeared on her communications repeater, and a subset of the main view screen shifted to receive the video link.

"Hot shit," she said, more than slightly incredulous, "he's picked up the call, time to see who we've been dealing with."

The blinking blue screen was replaced with the distorted image of a coarsely furred face, reminiscent of a flat-faced wolf atop a bony, bipedal body. A thick red mane ringed his canine face and his mouth was a horror show of tiny, razor teeth where it wasn't twisted by scars. Four eyes glared at her, the raw fervor evident in the maroon irises, or what passed for irises among the Dirregaunt. Beneath, his clawed hands rested upon two bone protuberances extruded from his chest. He waited, the time delay between the relays already several seconds. Beside the commander, presumably their XO, eyes split between the viewscreen and Best Wishes.

"Human Victoria. I must admit, you are not what I expected. So . . . soft . . . the color of last light. Could one such as you truly drag me across the stars as you have?"

Victoria stood from her command couch, knowing the camera followed her as she did. She stepped past Huian, closer to the view screen.

"Commander Best Wishes. I won't waste your time. You know I have the First Prince."

"Vick, he's at the second relay," hissed Avery over the open circuit. The display began to blink in her single functioning retinal implant. She had left out that she didn't want to waste time because she needed a deal before the *Springdawn* found her.

The Dirregaunt on her screen shook his mane, their version of a shrug. "And you know that I will find your vessel and destroy it, as I did the *Dreadstar*. You are a credit to the lesser empires, but these games grow tiresome."

"Third relay Vick,"

She swallowed. Best Wishes had betrayed no notion that he was aware his ship even followed the relay signals. She was running out of time fast.

"You also have one of my crew. A fighter, trapped in your ship."

"Fourth relay"

Victoria continued, "My government has ordered the surrender of the First Prince. I would like to exchange her for Tavram."

The Dirregaunt commander's head cocked slightly. "Your spacewalker murderess has Dirregaunt blood on her teeth," he said. His response came quicker than the last, the distance the signal had to travel greatly reduced.

"Fifth"

"Not as much as Prince Tavram. You can have him, *alive*, and at his volunteering on the condition we are allowed to ferry the rest of the Malagath to the frontier."

That seemed to startle the commander of the *Springdawn*. "The First Prince has . . . surrendered . . . *willingly*? To protect his pack?"

"Not very Malagath, is it?" asked Victoria.

"Sixth"

"I accept his surrender under the discussed conditions," said Best Wishes, reluctantly. His eyes had become vacant, his tone carried resignation, of all things. Victoria could understand it. She had taken the conclusion of a great hunt away from him. His duty warred with the primal need to slake the thirst for driving a hunt to completion. The commander's duty had won out, but it was a close thing if his sagging face was any indication. To work at something so long, only to have it handed to you at the moment of your triumph, unearned. It was draining. Conversely, she could see the XO relax, as though a weight had been lifted.

The proximity alarm went off as the *Springdawn's* tactical FTL drive brought the Dirregaunt within a few thousand meters of the gravitic buoy, all weapon batteries hot. Almost a half million kilometers away, the ion cloud blocked optical sensors, but her tactical display had superimposed a model of the *Springdawn*. *Gods but the ship was huge.* Alone it probably had more tonnage than half the privateer fleet.

"Conn sensors, two more contacts creeping up behind the buoy. Grayling cutters, from the looks."

"Sneaky fuckers . . ." Victoria muttered under her breath. If giving up the moment of triumph was draining, more-so was having to hand over your accomplishment to another who didn't deserve it. The Dirregaunt's deal with the Graylings probably involved handing her over in some regard. The Dirregaunt may not go so far as to protect her from the bugs, but she couldn't conjure Bargult looking favorably on the Dirregaunt commander's new resolution. She scanned the command repeaters. Carillo was already developing solutions for the new contacts. She looked back at the commander of the *Springdawn*.

"Human Victoria. I am not foolish enough to fall for this ploy. This is not your ship. I deal in good faith. Bring forth the Dirregaunt Prince. And where is your damnable space walker?"

Victoria watched through the bridge camera on the *Springdawn* as the hatch to the control room slid open, a dark silhouette filling the gap. She grinned, bearing her teeth at the supposed apex predator of the stars. "She's closer than you might think."

CHAPTER 11
THE CRUCIBLE

"CONN, SENSORS, THE Graylings are firing on the buoy."

Victoria verified the report on her display. The Dirregaunt may have been wise to the ploy, but the Graylings' sensor information would tell them they had caught the Vulture.

"Huian, take us past the *Springdawn*, increase acceleration and make for the system core."

The Dirregaunt cruiser drifted without power, its command center likely riddled with bullet holes now, but the Grayling cutters were under no such compunction, and soon they would realize their mistake. Hopefully Tessa Baum knew what she was doing.

"You think he always intended to feed us to Bargult?" Victoria mused, scanning her command repeaters. Sirens went off in the conn, drawing her attention back to the view screen. One of the Grayling cutters shattered, cut to scrap and ignited by the *Springdawn's* forward laser array. "I guess that's the end of that alliance," she said.

Victoria raised her voice to be heard over the open microphone. "Tac, hammer them both with the rail mines. And be ready, those aren't the only two cutters out here, not on your life."

The other six missiles the *Condor* had launched came online, the compact, ultra-light railguns tracked and fired on the remaining cutter and the *Springdawn*. They wouldn't do more than tickle the dreadnaught, but they would sure as hell confuse it. Hopefully it would buy them a little time as the *Springdawn* looked for the source of the attack.

The *Condor* tore a whirling vorticular tunnel through the brilliant ion cloud as Huian accelerated the ship towards the star. If they could just make it to horizon distance, they would reach the frontier of the Malagath Empire. *If Tessa Baum could just buy them that time.*

"Conn, engineering, Vick we've got a problem."

"Go ahead Yuri," said Victoria.

"This ion cloud is acting like thin atmo, it's heating up as we push through it, we're riding a pressure wave that's going to paint our coordinates across the sky like a bonfire. It's wearing through the forward ablative armor."

"Shit, and leaving a trail two thousand meters across. Push through it, we can't afford to take this slowly."

The hatch to the Conn slid open behind her.

"Captain Victoria!" said a voice somewhere near the ceiling. She had known this was coming, but had hoped to avoid it. One did not snub a Malagath prince, however.

Prince Tavram was dressed in one of the xeno vacuum suits, comically large for him. She had wanted him off the conn for the encounter with Best Wishes, so had sent him aft to wait for the transfer she never intended to make. It was tricky business, her gamble to play the Graylings off the Dirregaunt, and the Prince's presence might have influenced Best Wishes' decision.

"This is not a good time, Tav," she barked, but Tavram wasn't one to take no for an answer.

"Captain, I volunteered myself, and you have spat in

the face of our enemy after he accepted our surrender. You *humans* have a collective death wish; it's no wonder half the lesser empires are at your throat!"

She turned, rankled by his proximity and attitude. She pushed the slender xeno back, much to his surprise. He tripped into the XO's chair, from where his eyes were almost level with hers.

"Alright you royal xeno cocksucker, shut up and listen. One, no one talks to me like that on my ship. Two, I am the final authority out here, not some State and Colony puke half a billion miles away. Sorry Huian, I'm sure your mother's a great gal. *Three*, while your naïve newfound idealism is endearing, it's a death warrant for me and mine. What do you think your buddies on the frontier do to us when they find out we handed the heir to their empire over to the DG on their doorstep? I'll give you a fucking hint, it won't be pretty, and it won't be quick. But it did give me an idea, and idea on how to *maybe* get you home where that little seed of selflessness can *maybe* grow a tree of giving a fuck about someone other than yourself."

"Conn, sensors, Grayling contacts, two cutters inbound at a point-three, bears three-four-four on a positive azimuth."

Victoria turned away from the First Prince as her forward view screen highlighted and framed the two wicked-looking ships.

"*Tac,* bring the rails online."

Thunder filled the *Springdawn*, impossibly loud. Consoles and displays sparked and shattered as the space walker carpeted the bridge with her horrid, primitive weapon. The Grayling had been her first target, its neck ending in a greasy, cratered stump as it slumped over the railing of the observation ring. The human warrior leapt on top of the aft communication station and shakily swung her weapon in his direction. *How had she even gotten on the bridge?* The familiar stink of sulfur began to suffuse the air.

A sinister buzz and a solid-sounding thump drew Best Wishes' attention away from the human female. Modest Bearing held both hands buried in his mane, where wetness was beginning to soak through the filaments. His first officer had been hit. Best Wishes caught the wounded officer as he collapsed to his knees, pressing his back to a console to shield himself from further fire.

His security team had already begun to interpose between him and the space walker, who had begun moving about the bridge from cover to cover, firing blindly over consoles to keep his crew's heads down. Several other members of the security team surrounded him, pulling him towards the hatch.

"I'll not leave him," Best Wishes shouted over the din. The lead officer scowled, ears closed against the cacophony of the primitive's weapon. But he must have discerned Best Wishes' intent. He gestured to two of his men, who began to drag Modest Bearing along towards the forward hatch by his bloody mane and bony hooks. Best Wishes tried to look over the console, but the security officer shoved his head down, pushing him towards the hatch.

He cast one final look through the hatch as the security team shoved him down the passageway along with the other rescued members of the bridge crew. Dutiful Heiress looked at him with terrified eyes as she made to catch up with them, but spacewalker grabbed her from behind and threw her to the ground. Though the creature had no face save for a smooth black panel, he could feel the human's eyes on him as his security team slammed the hatch shut and smashed the control console, Dutiful still trapped within. Somehow the space walker could override their door controls, and permanently damaging them was the only way to make certain it couldn't follow in a timely manner. There were ways around, redundant paths wound through the *Springdawn* like a maze. It had never been designed to account for hostile warriors within the hull. Best Wishes' ears opened back up slowly as they retreated.

The security team's radioman said something to Kind Host. A lieutenant, he recalled. He was grateful his ears were still too muffled to hear the harsh radio waves so close to the source. He much preferred messengers to short-wave communicators. The lieutenant had to shout in his ear for him to hear the report. "We need to get you to the secondary command center, sir," said Kind Host, "The Grah'lhin have begun attacking the crew, and fired on what they believe to be the *Condor*."

The fools. He'd have given them the *Condor*. His arrangement with the human predicated no stipulation in regards to the Grah'lhin. As much as he reviled letting her bargain deprive him of cutting her ship from the stars, it was better to see her fall at the hands of even temporary hunting allies. Once he had the First Prince on board, Victoria would have been left to her own merit against the superior numbers of the Grayling ships.

Pushed through the hatch he could feel the ship's capacitors vibration translate through the decking. The forward laser battery had discharged, spilling luminous death into the ion cloud. *The Grah'lhin.*

The security detail pushed them through several winding passages, beginning to move towards the secondary command center at the foremost portion of the ship, where transparent alloys would offer a raw view of the outside space. Some of the team split his command crew towards a different route lest they all be ambushed together while the lieutenant led the way into an adjacent compartment. The chamber was lined with short, ruffled bactis stalks from the northern swamps on the home world. Course grass muffled their footfalls as they marched, but something was off. Best Wishes called a halt.

The bactis stalks were cultivated only within the outboard sections of the ship.

"Lieutenant, we're going the wrong direction. The auxiliary command center is that way," said Best Wishes, gesturing behind them.

The lieutenant's ears twitched as he glanced at the door and then to the officer supporting Modest Bearing. Best Wishes saw the unease in his eyes, and in turn the other members of the security team.

"I see."

The security team dropped Modest Bearing to the deck, where he tried to sit, but fell back. His pallid skin was a sharp contrast to his blood-soaked mane. The human's weapon had punched a hole in his first officer, just as the holes had been torn through Lightest Grove in the shuttle bay. Clean punctures, no burns or scoring. Just an empty void from where his blood spilled onto the grass. What kind of weapon could do such a thing so neatly?

The security officer that had dropped Modest Bearing raised his laser towards Best Wishes.

"Is this to be your legacy, Lieutenant? Betrayal of the highest order?"

Kind Host bared his rows of tiny razor-like teeth. "The betrayal belongs to you. Bringing those *things* on board, failing to kill the First Prince, and letting the lesser empires make fools of the Praetory. We'll not let you take us to the gates of the Malagath Empire to be destroyed for your obsession. There is consensus between those among the crew who matter. You must be removed if we are to survive," he said, raising his laser in turn.

Those among the crew who mattered. The upper castes, mindful only of status and power. They had lost the will for the hunt long ago and now cared only for their own comfort and advancement. Best Wishes looked into the laser's emitter, and then behind as the forest of bactis stalks began to quiver, as though something moved within.

"And so you have brought me here to murder me? Separated us from those still loyal who would not follow the perpetrators of such a cowardly deed."

"It's hardly murder. More akin to crushing an insect grown above his station."

"I rather think," said Best Wishes, as warm flecks of chitin began to glow to his top eye from behind the nearest of the tall stalks, "That you should worry more of overgrown insects crushing you."

A shrill cry brought Kind Host's attention back to the line of bactis, where two Grah'lhin erupted from the foliage, charging down the line of security officers. The pair struck the line of officers, stabbing with spear-like forelegs that jutted through the lieutenant at chest and stomach and lifted him from the deck. The team opened fire in panic with their handheld lasers even as they were struck down, killing the larger of the two even as it cleaved their numbers. Before they could focus fire on the last, both remaining Dirregaunt officers and Best Wishes were from their feet as a series of impacts rang through the hull, rattling the *Springdawn*. *Dead stars*, what was that?

Best Wishes twisted, reaching for a laser one of the

fallen officers had dropped as the last Grah'lhin cast aside the traitor's body and lumbered over him. He rolled, avoiding the stabbing claws that embedded themselves in the deck, and fired at the first joint, severing the foreleg. The Grah'lhin collapsed on him, scrabbling for purchase on the slick grass. Best Wishes claws flashed out, tearing away part of the retractable shield which protected the vulnerable sensory band. The Grah'lhin shrieked, trying to pull away, but Best Wishes dug his claws in and forced the active end of the emitter through the small opening.

"You're finished, filth. Tell all your kind," he spat. The creature shuddered and hissed as the handheld laser pistol discharged. The reek of burned bone scoured his nostrils, and a hot, greasy film began to drip from the sensory cavity.

The Grah'lhin spasmed a final time and collapsed on top of him, pain shooting up his leg as his knee wrenched from the weight. He looked to the side, gasping in pain. Modest Bearing's lifeless eyes stared back, blood seeping from the corner of his mouth. He had bled out during the firefight.

Best Wishes scanned his first officer, gut wrenching at the sorry state to which he had been reduced.

"Perhaps you were right, old friend. We should have turned towards home and stopped this mad chase. I have welcomed death aboard this vessel, and those who follow me taste it. But it is too late to turn back now."

Pain flared as the weight of the Grah'lhin's corpse was heaved off by the two remaining security officers, relieving the pressure on his lower body. His leg had been broken, twisted to an impossible angle. Above him, one of the security officers offered a hand. His face held something like awe at Best Wishes' ferocity in killing the Grah'lhin, the same ferocity that had earned him his command. "Not all of us are disloyal to you, Commander. Please, the hunt needs you."

It took considerable effort to loop his claws through one of the security officer's bone protuberances to stay upright.

He looked at the second officer. "And you?"

The Dirregaunt hesitated, glancing at the bodies around them. As his laser hand twitched, Best Wishes lifted his own and shot the disloyal crewmate dead. He scanned the faces of the bridge officers behind him, men he knew were true to him. They likely were to be killed as well, soon after himself.

They passed Kind Host on their way forward. It seemed some life yet clung to him as Best Wishes stepped over him, looking at the pitiful traitor. He raised his laser again, but stopped short of activating the emitter. Death would come as sure as the dawn for this one, there was no need to hurry his passing.

"Let's proceed," he said, leaving the security lieutenant to his painful end.

The hatch to the secondary command center was just forward of the belly gun targeting center, where it was clear the Grah'lhin had been previously. Best Wishes could smell the blood as they passed, but the remaining team had reached the secondary bridge without incident. Sliding the hatch open bathed the corridor in the iridescent light of the ion cloud. The remaining crew flinched back, shying away and closing their top eye to the hypnotic effects of the undulating infrared swirls. Best Wishes drank it in, letting it fill his senses until he felt as though the transparent paneling didn't exist at all, like he was exposed to the vacuum and one with the void.

"Take me in," he whispered, "The First Prince awaits us."

CHAPTER 12
HORIZON

TESSA STARED DOWN AT the quivering Dirregaunt female, pressed up against the bulkhead near the hatch the commander had escaped through. At least, she thought he was the commander, the security team had made an awful fuss about trying to protect him. He was blurry, but she thought he'd fit the description the dead courier gave him. She'd shot at him, but only managed to hit the taller one beside him. But she had seen the look on his face as she had accosted the female. The wide eyes, the open jaw. Loss was nearly universal, at least to xenos with expressive faces, mirrored by her own face when Aimes had taken out the primary communication array.

She wanted to kill the pitiful thing, so thin and waiflike. She wanted to kill all of them for chasing the *Condor* halfway across the Orion Spur, for scratching her up and giving her this fever and burning hip wound. But something in the way the commander had looked at this one. Could it be his mate? His lover? A sibling?

Tessa looked around, trying not to let the room spin. The bridge was filled with the dead and the cries of the dying. She had hit at least five, mostly collateral damage as she attempted to destroy as much of the navigation, intercommunication, and sensor aggregate equipment as she could.

The *Springdawn* had a redundant command center somewhere forward, but it would take time for Best Wishes to get situated and regain full control of his ship. Until then, Captain Marin could gain headway towards the solar core. Provided the Graylings didn't catch her first, though it looked like they had begun turning on the crew of the *Springdawn*. She hadn't expected that, but the chatter was unmistakable. That the Dirregaunt were using shortwave radios at all was telling. Radio waves were painful to Dirregaunt physiology, but the Graylings were making it too dangerous to use runners. With any luck the two xenos would have their hands too full of each other to bother with her.

Returning her attention to her new captive, Tessa took a knee beside the bulkhead, leaning on her rifle. With some luck it would mask her exhaustion and fever. The thump of her armored knee against the deck startled the Dirregaunt, who tried to scrabble as far away from her as possible into the corner of the *Springdawn's* bridge. To think humans were so cowed before these frightful creatures, just because the brain inside that head was capable of light speed calculations on the fly.

"Please," it whispered, "don't hurt me."

"Tell me your name, Dirregaunt," said Tessa. Her suit's onboard computer translated it to the Dirregaunt language before spitting it out the external speakers. The surviving member of the bridge crew whimpered, not expecting Tessa to know her language. Xenos were often put on edge by such mundane tricks, and even the Dirregaunt were no exception.

"I am Dutiful Heiress, spacewalker. Please, leave me."

Xeno superstitions more ancient than the human written word, and the Vultures fit them like a glove. Before the xeno could react, Tessa lashed out and snagged a handful of her mane.

"Why should I not just kill you now? What value does your life hold?" she asked, approximating what she hoped was a sinister tone in their language. It seemed to be doing the trick.

"My father is a Lord of the Hunt. I am heir to my family's holdings, seven planets and three mineral-rich moons. I alone am worth more than many lesser empires. I can make you wealthy."

Tessa slammed her fist into the bulkhead above Dutiful Heiress. She left it there, leaning on it for support. "What need have I of your planets and moons? I walk between stars," she snarled. In her mind she could picture Aimes sniggering at the melodramatic airs. "What value does your life hold *to me*?"

With no answer forthcoming Tessa climbed back to her unsteady feet, shouldering her rifle. As she lifted it the Dirregaunt shrieked again, holding her hands up defensively.

"Wait, please, I have value, I swear. The Commander, he harbors notions of a life as my mate."

That was more like it. Best Wishes' mistress could be a useful tool. Not that Tessa had any intention of executing the poor creature, but she didn't need to know that.

"These notions, what fruit do they bear?"

Dutiful sat up angrily, a defiant snarl twisting her mouth. "None," she said, "the Commander is of the lower caste. Skilled in the hunt perhaps, but he has no prospect of ever mating me. He is beneath my station. He will never have anything than command of a small clutch. But his base desires will elevate me."

Tessa huffed. What a stone-cold bitch. So much for pack loyalty, everyone on board this ship seemed to resent their commander in one way or another. Still, unrequited affection might also buy the Vultures a few more precious minutes to make a horizon jump. A not altogether healthy idea of vengeance tickled her mind at taking something that Best Wishes loved, even if it was one-sided.

"Come on," said Tessa, grabbing a handful of the Dirregaunt's mane, "You're going to show me where this secondary bridge is."

———

"Missiles away, Vick"

As if she couldn't see the goddamn things on the view screen, tearing through the ion cloud on a contrail of vibrant, burning plasma as the range on the Grayling cutters chewed through an alarming number of kilometers.

"Huian, roll us over and dive down, see if we can't confuse this wake a bit," said Victoria. The false horizon twisted and dropped below the view-screen as the *Condor* went perpendicular to the stellar plane. She referenced her tactical repeater, watching the cutters swoop down to stay between her and the star. *Shit,* they knew what she was about. The cloud churned behind her as momentum continued carrying her towards the cutters. Bargult was slowing to match her relative velocity, even as the missile volleys carved a path towards his two cutters.

"Conn, Tac. Twelve seconds to impact on the primary."

"Light up the rails, try and sneak it through their point defense while they're busy with the missiles," she ordered.

The relative motion of the cutters and the *Condor* would reduce the Grayling's window to deal with new attacks as light took time to reflect off the *Condor* and bounce to the cutters, but they were quickly closing into a range at which light-delay tactics would become almost nil. Graylings preferred the up-close kill.

"Solution locked, firing as she bears . . . firing."

The lights dimmed as power funneled to the twin magnetic drivers running the length of the ship. A spray of tungsten bolts erupted from the front of the shuddering *Condor,* accelerated faster than any missile and small enough to be missed by most sensors. But Bargult was a familiar enemy, and even if the Grayling didn't understand projectile weapons, he'd sure learned to fear their bite.

"The primary is maneuvering, Vick."

Bargult knew what it meant when the *Condor's* bow swung towards him, even during what should seem like a benign trajectory adjustment.

Her screen flashed. That maneuvering had cost him his point-defense precision. He wasn't exactly torn to pieces by the rail guns, but two of the six missiles she'd fired had made it close enough to damage him. It looked like a second star flaring briefly in the cloud, a corona that must be distressingly close to be visible without magnification.

He was out of the fight with that ship for now, but not dead yet. Worse still, Bargult had used the opportunity to close the distance between the *Condor* and the second cutter. Every maneuver Victoria made was a calculated sacrifice, trading precious range for careful positioning and opportunities to hit back.

"Huian, level us out, all ahead and put our dorsal plating towards his first salvo."

The ship spun again, the flat, shrouded disc of the star centering on the view-screen as the *Condor* continued to push towards the core of the system.

"Conn, Tac, the secondary is on a parabolic intercept, we have a solution that might shake up his course."

"Tactical, you have the rails, and send out the last of our

new toys," said Victoria as the cutter's arc was highlighted on her view screen. Her pilot surrendered the controls momentarily as her tactical team nudged the *Condor* into position and fired another volley of tungsten slugs amidst another three missiles. One containing electric chaff exploded in between the *Condor* and the intercept path. The other small missiles sped out ahead of the *Condor*.

The Grayling correctly anticipated the attack, and increased their acceleration to avoid the invisible hailstorm of metal shards. Smart buggers, but the first of the two missiles was spreading chaff across their new intercept path.

"Here he comes, Huian," said Victoria, "load the evasion program."

The Grayling cutter emerged from a thick bank of the ion cloud, screaming towards the *Condor* on a similar wake of superheated gas. Victoria increased the magnification on the view screen, and could see the prongs of the cutter's deadly arc throwers sparking to life.

Plasmic lightning tore across the gulf between the two ships, tendrils snapping and igniting small pockets of flammable vapors along the path before biting into the cloud of conductive chaff. The *Condor* bucked as the rail guns fired again, the projectiles turning red-hot as they passed through the Grayling barrage. The first arcs of lightning began to lick the hull of the *Condor* as the cutter burned through the chaff buffer. Warnings blared as the ablative plating was stripped away.

"Huian, turn us about, military acceleration, past the dampers," said Victoria. She thumbed the general circuit on her command console as she secured her harness. "Crew, prepare for emergency acceleration."

A low rumble engulfed the *Condor* as the ion engines drove her beyond the limit of the inertial dampers' ability to react. Black spots crowded the edge of her vision as she was pressed against the command couch by the g-forces.

"Conn, sensors." It was Avery, sounding every bit as labored as she felt. "The secondary is breaking positive azimuth to avoid the chaff, increasing acceleration to catch up and dropping his evasion program to save speed. He's gaining fast."

"Conn, Tac. We're ready to send a few punches back at him on your mark."

"Negative, tactical, he'll wipe anything with a heat sig we try to shove down his throat. Start a solution for the rails."

"Vick, he'll see the rails coming a mile away, and if we spin like that he'll fry us."

"Not those rails, Tac."

There was a brief pause on the circuit, punctuated only by the steady beeping of her command console, alerting her each time the cutter gained ten kilometers on them.

"Copy, Vick. Working on a solution, stand by."

If they didn't all pass out first. She looked towards the First Prince. He didn't seem to be doing well, the Malagath had evolved past the need for g-force tolerances. For all she knew this could be lethal levels for some of his crew. She swore. This was all for nothing if she killed the damn prince herself. She had no choice.

"Huian, cut the acceleration down to nominal levels."

Victoria's primary helmsman turned to look at her, but caught sight of Tavram in the XO's chair, realizing what was happening. The thundering inferno behind them lessened to a dull roar and the beeping became even more frequent.

"Conn, sensors, he's charged again."

"Chaff away," said Victoria.

Too late, her rear view screen was washed out by the

white-hot lightning stretching across the hundreds of kilometers separating the ships. It was silent for a moment, then the plasmic arcs struck the *Condor* from behind. The hull of the ship screamed as the Grayling weapon stripped layers of metal and reactive armor from the fantail of the privateer ship. A hollow snap ripped through the length of the *Condor* as the acceleration cut and the ship began to spin wildly, spewing brilliant xenon into the cloud in an ever-increasing spiral.

"Conn, engineering, he took out the primary engine," Yuri called over the circuit. The rough, patchy call was cut off by a burst of static.

She'd picked up on that. The view-screen stabilized as the computer compensated for the spin, and focused on the Grayling cutter. It followed a straight trajectory towards her ship. *Graylings liked the up-close kill.*

"Conn, Tac. We have the solution."

"Fucking fire, then!"

The other two missiles she'd launched with the initial electric chaff came on line. The last Doberman rail mines that she'd labored to eclipse with her own ship fired their deadly payload.

The Grayling cutter stopped his evasive maneuvering during the mad acceleration, and hadn't resumed it upon disabling the *Condor*. Now two lengths of ballistic tungsten, holy spears from the gods of war, tore past the *Condor*. They narrowly avoided the forward edge of the ship in its wild spin.

Bargult never saw it coming. How could he? In this world of defense sensors built to detect laser batteries and particle cannons, gravitic distortions and propulsion spectrum analysis, what dirty, primitive fools would hurl unguided lengths of metal at something so tiny as a moving ship hundreds of kilometers away?

The two projectiles took his ship just forward of the weapons systems, at relative speeds far beyond the hypersonic threshold. Barbs extended from the projectiles as they struck, turning each one into bevy of giant's knives striking with almost incomprehensible kinetic force. Everything aft of the cutter's nosecone shattered, disintegrated in an instant. The ruined engines of the cutter vented hot plasma, which engulfed the cutter as it ignited. What little remained was swallowed by the roiling inferno that followed.

Vick swallowed, watching the last pieces of shrapnel scatter to the depths of space. Even a temporary reprieve was welcome, but there was no time to dally.

"Skipper," Huian called from the pilot's station, "I've got almost no control."

"Do what you can to get us straightened out. Engineering, conn, what's your status? I'm showing more red shit on my screen than a low-budget slasher."

Static

"Engineering, conn. Respond."

"Conn, engineering, this is Cohen. Lieutenant Denisov is dead. He tried to disconnect the Alcubierre, but it blew when the Grayling fried us."

So it had been his last tour after all. God rest the bastard, he'd kept the Vultures flying better than any chief engineer she'd ever had.

"So we're dead in the water. No main engine, no FTL."

"We've still got the Horizon, Skipper."

Victoria pressed the heel of her hand to her forehead. "This far from the star it might as well be scrap too. The rate we're moving it would take us over a day to get to jump distance. We don't have a day. We don't even have an hour."

There was chatter on the other end of the engineering circuit, and the feedback of a hand rubbing against the microphone. A moment later Cohen came back on the circuit, "Captain, Aurea says she might have a solution."

"The *Malagath*?" asked Victoria. She cast a glance at Tavram, sitting nearby, and looking worse for wear after the high G-forces. Hell, that was an understatement, the xeno looked half dead. He was only semi-conscious, but he was recovering.

Another shriek of feedback grit her teeth before a high lilting voice took over on the circuit. "Human Captain Victoria. You may recall I mentioned a piece of your equipment was functionally similar to that of the *Dreadstar's*."

Was she rigging up a Malagath weapon back there? Yuri had said he barely recognized the GSD after her tinkering. "At this point, I'm willing to try anything."

"Conn, sensors. Whatever you're trying, try it quick or not at all. I've got the damaged cutter back on the scope, headed straight for us.

Best Wishes swam in the ether as the *Springdawn* plunged through the ionic cloud, drinking in the richness of the colors with his top eye. The rest of his command crew had blinded themselves to the wonder, squinting shut their connection to the void. They had willfully blinded themselves to the hunt. Best Wishes could not even remember why.

Somewhere beyond that thin shroud of translucent alloy was the *Condor* and his prey. Here on the doorstep of Malagath space she had led him. Human. Victoria. These were the only words that held meaning for him anymore. She had tried to cheat him, tried to escape him, tried to *kill* him. Her, a filthy, primitive, lesser empire captain.

"Take us deeper," he whispered to no one in particular.

"You've already gone too deep," said a voice beside him. In his periphery, his first officer stood with a blood soaked mane. Best Wishes whipped his head around, but only the new head of his security team stood at his flank.

"Yes, Commander?"

His eye was closed. Blind fool. Where had Modest Bearing gone? Best Wishes turned back to the ion cloud, brilliant infrareds twirling as they parted around the hull of the *Springdawn*.

"Commander, we have a radiological trace, a weapons discharge closer to the star some minutes ago."

A nuclear missile. Such primitive, inelegant wastefulness. All that energy, and only a fraction of it set to purpose on its target.

"Then you have your heading, helmsman."

The cloud blurred as the *Springdawn's* faster-than-light drive closed the astral distance in the blink of an eye.

"Commander, the *Condor* is drifting without power, the last Grah'lhin ship is approaching it."

"Destroy the traitorous vermin."

The forward batteries hummed as a lance of energy carved a fiery hole through the cloud, enveloping the cutter even as it sliced the small craft from bow to stern.

"Fore batteries charging. Shall I destroy the *Condor* as well? Or have you come to your senses?"

Best Wishes turned to the weapons console. Modest Bearing stood before it, bathed in the infrared glow of the ion cloud. His eyes stared lifelessly at Best Wishes.

The commander shut his eyes to clear the vision. "Open a line of communication to the human vessel."

CHAPTER 13
THE DREADSTAR'S LEGACY

Victoria stared in disbelief at the figures Cohen was sending to her command station.

"That Malagath girl tinkered our stealth device into an emergency engine. Holy shit."

First Prince Tavram scanned the display over her shoulder, green light flashing on his face each time the last Grayling cutter closed another ten-thousand kilometers. The bugger was staying well-clear of their spin trajectory, taking no chances with her rail guns.

"The principle is sound, Captain Victoria," said Tavram. He extended a long, slender finger towards the display. "It would appear as though the original technology, though primitive in nature, has origins in Malagath science. Adapted to an unknown number of purposes by various lesser empires. The original purpose beyond their capabilities. Not, however, beyond mine."

Victoria was getting desperate, but the amount of power required to replicate the effects of the emergency engine was nearly incalculable by human standards. Gravity manipulation was still a rudimentary science, and a decent chunk of reactor power funneled straight into the artificial gravity and inertial dampeners. Creating a body massive enough to brush horizon space, even for a fraction of a second, would take everything the *Condor* had left to give. The math required to execute such a horizon jump was not just incalculable, but practically incomprehensible.

"Cohen, get Aurea what she needs to make it happen. We'll get one shot at this. It'll melt the cabling."

"That's if we're lucky, Captain. It might even rupture the reactor containment."

And then Bargult would be eating fried Vulture for dinner. "Set it up," said Victoria. She looked up at the pilot's station. "Huian, plot it. Cohen should have already sent you the specifics."

"I've been trying, Ma'am, but the computer can't handle all the variables, it's slowing down to a crawl trying to compute the horizon jump solution."

The First Prince rolled his shoulders, a Malagath display of amusement. "This is precisely why such calculations should not be left to computers," he said. He gestured to the pilot's station. "Captain?"

"Huian, move it."

First Prince Tavram slid behind the helm as Victoria's pilot retreated, legs splayed awkwardly. His slender blue fingers flew across the console, practically blurring in their frantic speed. The skin folds on his neck opened, venting heat to cool the excess blood flowing into his brain as he began to perform the necessary calculations required for transdimensional travel. "I shall require a few minutes, Victoria."

They didn't have them, the Grayling cutter was already shifting to match their momentum, the green flashes on her tactical repeater registering more slowly with each passing cycle.

Stall.

"Avery, get him on the horn."

"Who?"

"Who the *fuck* do you think? Get that ugly bug on my screen before I put your head through a fucking sensor stack!"

The *Condor's* optics enlarged the cutter as the obscuring veil of the ion cloud thinned. Wicked arcs of electricity crawled across the jagged red resin skin of the cutter, igniting small pockets of volatile gas as the Grayling ship passed them.

"Signal coming through, Vick. Audio only."

"Put it through," said Victoria. The First Prince continued to work furiously, balancing the space-time pull of stars in his complex mind.

There was silence for a moment in the conn, but for the furious taps of slender blue fingers, before a deep chittering filtered through the newly opened circuit. Bargult had no true face, and so felt no need to show one at all. His ship could interface directly with his consciousness, and so give voice to the formless xeno as well as any of his manifold bodies.

Victoria shuddered, her skin felt like insects crawled up and down every inch of raised gooseflesh.

"Human . . . Victoria . . ."

The name was drawn out, being tasted, *savored*. This was a Grayling that knew it held fresh prey pinned in its claws, and no amount of missiles could dissuade those creepers of lightning from reaching across the blank kilometers of space to scour the *Condor's* hull. The same creepers would penetrate the ship and quickly fry the brains and hearts of every last Vulture onboard, if they were lucky. Otherwise reactive armor would boil away into space and the molecular bonds of the steel and composite hull would dissolve into slag, venting atmosphere and crew to vacuum.

"Bargult. You've lost three ships to run me down. Was it worth it?"

"A heavy price. I am diminished, hanging by mere strands. But I am victorious. Ships can be rebuilt, new bodies incubated and integrated, but a human prize once lost is not easily won a second time, as you have so shown."

"And the Dirregaunt? You've made enemies of them."

The buzzing on the circuit intensified, she resisted the urge to claw at her ears.

"The Dirregaunt betrayed us. We were to share you, but the commander would withdraw from our bargain. His will for the hunt was weak."

"And you just couldn't bear to see us go, you ugly fucking creeper. You've got an unhealthy obsession with humans, Bargult."

"We all have our vices, Human Victoria."

Her response was interrupted as an alert flashed on her command repeater. She thumbed the mute switch for the ship-to-ship circuit.

"Avery, what is it?"

"Photon Doppler. Superluminal contact, Vick. Outboard the star, *Springdawn* inbound!"

She looked at the First Prince, deep in a trance-like state as his mind continued to balance numbers that would have given her ship's computer an aneurism. He needed more time.

Victoria took her finger from the mute switch. Before she could say anything to the chittering Grayling, the line shrieked and went dead. On the view screen she picked out the telltale sign of laser fire, and the smaller Grayling cutter detonate as the engine compartment was compromised.

"Thus ends Bargult . . ." she whispered. The Dirregaunt didn't mess around.

"Incoming comm signal, *Springdawn.*"

"Put it on," said Victoria. "I'm just Ms. Popular today," she muttered.

She shielded her eyes as the Dirregaunt commander replaced her view of the ion cloud, the entire screen bathed in the glaring red light of the sun's glow that her ship's optical sensors had toned down. A moment later the view screen adjusted, looking so much like the red wash of a darkroom.

"Human Victoria," said the commander of the *Springdawn.* No appreciable light-delay here, he was only a hundred thousand kilometers away, watching her spin helplessly through space from the bridge of one of the most advanced ships in the galactic neighborhood. Well within the range and scope of his laser batteries. Secondary bridge, she noticed, grinning. It looked as though Tessa Baum raised some hell. Pity she hadn't killed the bastard, but Victoria knew it was her own fault she let the Grayling tag the *Condor*, Tessa couldn't have stopped it by putting a bullet into Best Wishes.

"Commander, I must say, you're looking somewhat worse for wear," she said.

It was true, and not just as a result of the strange lighting. He appeared to be in some sort of fever fugue, the remainder of his bridge crew all seemed somewhat agitated as well. The Dirregaunt bared his mouthful of razor teeth at her.

"We had an accord, space walker. You fled with the First Prince. With my prize."

"Hold on now, champ. You broke that pact when the Graylings fired on us. You should have kept your pets on a leash."

"The Grah'lhin are dust. Their entire empire is worth less than dust. We both know the price I paid for my arrogance, and what you have taken from me."

Victoria cast a side-long glance at her idle helmsman. The young woman shrugged back at her, just as much at a loss for his meaning as Victoria herself. On her screen there was a brief superluminal alarm as the *Springdawn* enveloped itself in a shell of warped space-time and shunted towards the *Condor*.

Tactical Alcubierre, she noted. Victoria considered it a success if they came out of FTL less than two thousand klicks off their target destination. The *Springdawn* was nothing less than a ballet dancer, gracefully leaping from point to point with near-perfect precision. What she wouldn't give for that technology as she watched the dreadnought appear to grow rapidly on her screen, knowing the approach speed was skewed by her sublight perception. Even were her faster-than-light drive active, the Dirregaunt could slip ahead of her and shred her ship with ease.

"Even now, human Victoria, I am tempted to board your vessel and take my prize in person. Would such be folly? Two of your kind have taken so much from me. How many of these warrior caste do you have waiting, gnashing their teeth at the prospect of Dirregaunt flesh?"

"Come find out. How many Dirregaunt does it take to plug an airlock?"

A low, rasping growl hummed over the open circuit. "I am not quite so unwise, human. Whichever god or devil spewed forth your vicious kind will greet you now."

"Wait," she said, grasping for any tactic to delay him, "Don't you want the fucking First Prince alive?"

"No longer."

"What about Dutiful Heiress?"

Whatever Best Wishes had been about to say stammered and died in his throat. "What?" he demanded, still aglow with the thick, red light.

The *Springdawn* was so close that Red had reestablished two-way communications with Tessa Baum, and she had quite a few interesting things to say. Namely about the Commander's extracurricular interests inside his command.

"Take a look in the corridor, Commander."

———

Best Wishes shook. The human female on his screen warped and undulated as she spoke, at times resembling the faceless nightmare prowling his ship, at others bearing a passable and inexplicable similarity to his first officer. Hailing her ship had been a mistake. He should have fired upon her and been done with it. But the order was caught in his throat every time he tried to give it.

To his back was the long corridor they had come by, closed now. He turned away from screen. The door seemed to drift towards him, though he had yet to take a step towards it. He reached out to stop himself from colliding with it.

"Show me," he growled.

His security officer looked at the remaining command staff, uneasy. "Don't look at them, look at me," he shouted. He hadn't intended to raise his voice, but it had the desired result. The officer waved a hand in front of the control unit for the door, turning a thin slice of the alloy transparent.

The spacewalker loomed into view, startling his command staff back. Handheld masers raised. A red glint reflected in the highlights of the creature's featureless black mask. The human warrior retreated, shoving a captive Dirregaunt in its place. A rough hand buried itself in the poor crewmember's main, wrenching the face up to the transparent wedge. Modest Bearing stared back at him with lifeless eyes through the sealed door.

He recoiled. "No," he said.

"Yes," came the voice behind him. The human bitch. Best Wishes stumbled to the door, twisted leg aching, fists slamming into the hard alloy. Blood, almost black in the harsh red light, still soaked the mane of his oldest friend. Drips fell from matted strands of hair, from the vicious hole the spacewalker had torn in his throat. Bile dripped from his teeth as the corpse of his First Officer opened its mouth to speak.

"How far will you take us, Commander? How much more will you sacrifice?"

"We are at an end, old friend, there is nothing left to give. No further cost."

"Is there not?" asked Modest Bearing, as his visage began to waver. His face narrowed, the mane became sleek and silken, the ears long and slender. Dead eyes filled with life and fear as the frightened face of Dutiful Heiress shimmered in the red light. His heart seized for a moment, tensing. *Was she dead too?*

"She'll remain unharmed, as long as the *Condor* is allowed to leave the system." *The voice behind him again. What did she speak of?* She could not leave, and she could not kill the dead a second time.

"Praetor guide me," he whispered. "Prepare to fire."

The tip of the human's weapon was being shoved roughly into the back of Dutiful Heiress' head, the creature clearly prepared to activate the weapon. He imagined one of those gaping holes spreading across her forehead.

"What have I done? Praetor, only my duty,"

I am beyond duty, now.

Best Wishes looked around the command center. No

one was moving. "I said prepare to fire!" he barked. Slowly, the bridge officers began to move. He turned away from the door, muffled cries of panic muted by the thick alloy. Not even the human could get through that blast door. Outside the *Springdawn* he could clearly see the tiny speck of the human ship, spinning helplessly in the red bask of the ion cloud. On the screen its captain bared her teeth at him.

"You'd let her die?" she asked.

"She's already dead, Human Victoria. You seek to take her from me twice? We are done talking."

"Shit, ok, fine, I'll release her, show of good faith."

The hunt is my faith. "End the communication," he said to the Broadcast Officer.

"Wait!" shouted the human captain. Best Wishes cast her one more wary glance.

"If you won't talk to me, at least talk to him," she said. Her optical sensor shifted down, revealing a tall blue figure manning one of her crew's stations. *Him.* Fury poured through his veins, his growls drowning the silence in the command center. *The First Prince.*

"Best Wishes," said Tavram, First Prince of the Malagath Empire.

———

Tenacity? Admirable, yet each of the human captain's gambits to dissuade the hunter had failed. Quite natural, such a primitive empire could not hope to contend with the likes of the Malagath or the Dirregaunt. The First Prince's war had extended millennia prior to his birth, a burning swath of galactic stalemates that had watched countless lesser empires rise and fall in its duration.

Here, Tavram could begin to put an end to it. Here, he juggled the weight of stars in his mind for the *Condor's* haphazard new emergency engine, and the weight of a war that had cost billions of lives.

"Hello, Commander."

Best Wishes stared back at him through the optical recorders. Insane? Clearly. The physiological symptoms were painted upon his face, his posture, his voice. Whether the pressure of the hunt had driven him to madness, or some other ailment the First Prince could not say. It was then no wonder that the human, Victoria could no reason with him. Perhaps the Dirregaunt hunter had always been insane? It had been said that the daughter of boldness and madness was genius, the commander of the *Springdawn* was surely that.

"So," hissed the Dirregaunt, "this is the face of a coward, hiding among the lesser empires. The *human* has kept you well hidden, but not well enough. You and your good shepherds go no further. I know not what brought you here, but no more blood will stain your hull."

"Peace is why I am here, Commander. The purpose of my mission, armistice between Malagath and Dirregaunt," said Tavram. The rattling numbers in his head wound down as he entered the data into the strange computer system of the *Condor*. He could activate the new emergency engine now, charge a singularity for a fraction of a second and use it to jump to Malagath space. They were so close now. But he stayed his hand, interested, ever the scholar.

"Peace?" growled Best Wishes, "From the murderer of millions? Where was your peace when the Sixth Fleet surrendered? Your broadside batteries cut them from the sky. Where was your *peace* when the Kossovoldt appeared in the Blackstar Nebula? Dirregaunt ships boiled as Kossovoldt plasma burned through metal and flesh, and what few escaped found the open net of your particle cannons waiting for them."

"It has to stop somewhere, these old hates. Does it not matter that your superior turned on the Praetory? I was to meet the Lords of the Hunt. We, each of us, were betrayed."

A quiet calm stole across the commander's features momentarily, before the twitches and tics returned.

"We are a long way from the Praetory, Prince. The hunt now is you and I."

Whatever madness had stolen reason from the Dirregaunt Commander would cost him his life. Tavram would have no better luck than the captain of the *Condor* with this madman. The *Springdawn* was close. So close that Tavram had figured the weight of the ship into the emergency engine calculations. Not mere child's play, even for him. His brain still burned from the effort. He would have liked to forge the beginnings of a truce here and now, but the Dirregaunt Commander would not have it. Unfortunate? Truly. The word of Best Wishes carried more weight than he knew among the Malagath.

"So be it," said First Prince Tavram as he activated the emergency engine.

The small ship went silent, lights flickering out and displays darkening as power was rerouted. Even the hiss of the ventilation quieted for a moment, before a high-pitched keen began to mount through the vibrating floor.

Before the main view screen went dead, Tavram watched the *Springdawn* lurch forward, twisting as the gravity field expanded. Its forward lasers blazed to life, the shafts warping around the building singularity in a multitude of curved, crawling lances. Behind the forward batteries Tavram could see the hull of the *Springdawn* buckle, rippling waves of alloy and composite tearing away among white geysers of atmosphere venting to vacuum.

The forward third of the dreadnaught sheared off as a cascade of debris fell towards the center of the artificial star. A final surge of power darkened even the main view-screen, and the keen turned to a thunderclap that shook the ship like a meteor impact.

The residual vibrations faded after a moment. The familiar growl of the *Condor's* primitive interstellar drive emerged from the tumult and the total darkness. He could hear another sound behind it, the rasping breath of the Human, Victoria, and the squeak of skin on synthetic fabric as she released the death-grip on her command couch.

"Horizon jump successful; course looks dead-nuts for . . . not Kallico'rey. What do your people call that star you pointed us at?" she asked. How she could verify his course in total darkness, without power to the bridge he was uncertain. Tavram collapsed into the cramped chair of the navigation station. He felt as though he had run the circumference of a gas giant. The familiar pain at the base of his brain he associated with the void behind the void crept back to greet him.

"To the Malagath, it is called the Eye of Salvation," said Tavram, massaging the top of his neck.

"No shit?"

"No shit, Human Victoria."

EPILOGUE

"WHATEVER ELSE HAPPENS, Captain Marin, I just wanted to say thank you. Thank you for keeping my daughter safe."

Alice Wong was speaking to Victoria Marin's back. The privateer captain was leaning against the window, watching the gentle rain patter the hardened glass. The colony of Ithaca had just entered the months-long wet season that would flood the deltas and fertilize the crops of the 400,000 citizens.

"Just Victoria, Madam Secretary. I don't hold the notion of keeping my captaincy."

Alice set down her coffee. "No? You brought back modern Malagath parts, not to mention a functioning emergency engine that one of their crew managed to assemble in your engine room."

"Yeah, Tech Div ripped it out almost before we docked. The usual drivel about security and proprietary knowledge. In any case, I disobeyed a direct order to get it here. I provoked the Dirregaunt and took the First Prince home."

"Strangely, no record of any such order exists, Victoria."

Alice couldn't contain a small smile as the gruff face of Victoria Marin turned toward her. She wasn't fond of the woman, but she'd put a black eye on Samson by defying an illegal order he had coerced Alice into sending.

"It seems that my crypto account was corrupted, all records of outgoing FTL communications are damaged beyond repair. Unless you want to go out to Pilum Forel and print out a hard copy to bring back. As far as I'm concerned, you never saw the orders, and neither did Captain Jackson. And since the final decisions involving privateer command are up to State and Colony . . ."

The perplexed expression turned sour, "Sammy's tampering in xeno politics now? That absolute asshole. I knew you'd never order us to hand over Tavram yourself." *Tavram?* Just how familiar with the Malagath prince had Victoria Marin gotten?

"Unfortunately there's no evidence of it, or of his influence in placing Huian on the *Condor* to use as leverage against me. You'll be pleased to know that my daughter is no longer attached to your ship. She'll be leaving Ithaca in a week for a navigator's billet aboard the *Clarke*."

"Huh," said Victoria. She turned back to the window, looking out over the space port. The captain was silent for a time. She finally said, "If I'm keeping the *Condor*, I hate having my crew mucked with by politicians. Huian's good on the pilot's bench, she's got a place if she wants it."

Another brief silence passed as Alice Wong considered it. She wasn't sure she could handle her daughter permanently aboard a privateer ship, amid all the danger of a hostile alien galaxy. Piracy patrol, colony defense, and interplanetary drug interdiction weren't glamorous, but they were safe. She opened her mouth to refuse Victoria, then stopped. Solicitations for privateer billets were rare in coming. Could she deny Huian such an opportunity?

"I'll consider your offer and pass that along next time I see her, Captain. Now, between you and me, what happened at the Eye of Salvation?"

Victoria Marin took one last glance out the window, where a freighter was launching with supplies for the orbital station. She watched it rise upward, the low rumble of its engines vibrating the glass in its fixture. Maybe it was carrying supplies to repair the *Condor*, somewhere up there in dry-dock.

"You know it's been over three years since I've seen rain?" she asked. She settled in to the chair opposite Alice with a grunt, sniffing at her cup of tepid local coffee.

"Not much to tell, Madam Secretary. We floated for three days before the Malagath picked up our distress call. Managed to get the maneuvering thrusters back so the spinning stopped making us all sick. They picked us up in this giant crate, made our colonial defense hulks look like one of my model star fighters. They kept us on that thing for another two days while they hauled the rescues and the First Prince out of system and checked the ion cloud. Not much left of the *Springdawn*, I guess. Just fragments, blown to every which hell"

"The Prince thanked us, before he left. Set some engineers to help with the repairs, under that rescue that built the drive, but we didn't hear from him again after they took him off ship. When we were spaceworthy, they vented the compartment and kept us under close guard all the way to the star for a jump. Then the Malagath kicked us out as soon as we got power back to the Horizon drive. I half-figured Cohen would mutiny and try to jump ship when that Malagath girl finally said goodbye and stepped off the *Condor*. We made best time here, the Jenursa made sure the road was smooth I think. Got brought planet-side and I've been here near a week now."

"A whole week with dirt under your heels and

non-recycled air in your lungs? You must be burning up."

Victoria grimaced. "It's the flat horizons that get to me, half my view blocked by a planet under my feet."

Alice lifted her tablet, cycling through her messages to the *Condor's* maintenance report she had been forwarded earlier that morning.

"Well Captain, in that case I imagine you'll be eager to see how the repairs are progressing on your ship."

First Prince Tavram strode through crystalline gates, the light of his home system's star refracted across the visible spectrum upon him and his guards as he entered the royal palace. Inexplicably, the wide hallways and arched ceiling made him long for the cramped, corroded passageways of the *Condor*.

The concourse stretched before him, composite pillars branching into a latticework that stretched into the clouds above. No rain ever fell in the palace, a charged net within the lattice structure wicked away the droplets before they could touch the ground. Opulence? More so, it seemed, than usual. Perhaps his time with the humans had humbled him somewhat. Not that it was inappropriate for the imperials to display this wealth of technology and power. But the servants and citizens falling prostrate as he passed had never before made him feel so . . . conscious . . . before. It had always been the proper way of things, both of the Malagath and the lesser empires.

Would the humans ever bow to me? Their histories mentioned such concessions, but I can imagine Victoria bending to no one. He stopped, spinning a slow circle.

"My Prince, your father awaits, and we should not dally."

His entourage, eyes similarly downcast, a mix of body-guards, politicians, and ship's captains hoping to gain favor with the Emperor for having ferried him home. They thought themselves noble heroes for having carried him the final miles after the humans bled and sacrificed for him. It was one of those captains that spoke. The captain that had brought the *Condor* aboard for repairs.

"Of course," he said, "let's not keep the Emperor waiting."

They climbed a small hill to the crown of the Malagath Empire, the center of a thousand worlds that stretched across the local cluster of stars. He had never felt such a massive sense of scale before being forced to hunch through the tiny hatches of the *Condor*, and now he craned his neck as they entered the royal court. More flawless crystal rimmed the hall, twisting, climbing spires creating a faceted forest that framed the throne. Thousands packed the floor and balconies, just as he'd always remembered, kneeling in a wave as they noticed his entrance. They came from every corner of the Malagath Empire, now represented in the palace on Malagan.

His father overshadowed the lot of them, atop a perfectly cut crystal throne and dressed in a tightly tailored uniform.

"You're back early," he said. His voice was repeated through amplifiers placed throughout the hall. Never one to mince words, was the Emperor.

"There were complications," said Tavram. The sonic sensors hovering nearby carried his voice, and probably the sound of his nervousness, directly through the throne.

The Emperor stood, the platform buzzing as it generated a significant amount of stairs for him to descend. Tavram recalled his father's explanation, that if you could not climb to the throne beneath the weight of the crown you did not deserve to sit in it. It would not be long before he no longer could, and then the Emperor would retire and the crown would pass to Tavram.

"All of you, out," the Emperor declared, "I speak with the Prince alone."

A loud rustle filled the hall as the thousands of blue faces shuffled past Tavram, his small following glancing back longingly at their vain chance for glory as they retreated from the chamber. He could have told them the Emperor would care little for their petty claims.

The colossal doors closed behind the crowd with a gesture from the Emperor. Out of the public eye, Tavram went to him, folding into the Emperor's open embrace. The emperor of a thousand worlds, the scourge of the galactic arm, the hand behind billions of lives governed and deaths dealt. His father.

"When we learned of the ambush I feared the worst. I thought the Dirregaunt had swept you from the stars. To find you alive and before me again is beyond words. Surely now you can give up this folly idea of peace? The ambush proves the Dirregaunt are not interested."

Tavram broke away from the Emperor, bowing his head in refute. "It proves the opposite, there is division in the Praetory. Those that sent Best Wishes are terrified, afraid that some among the Lords of the Hunt will entertain the idea of armistice. This was not an attempt on the life of the First Prince on behalf of the Praetory, this was an unsanctioned attack on the prospect of peace."

Breath hissed from between the Emperor's teeth. "*He* led the attack? *Dead stars*, how did you evade him all the way back to Malagath space?"

Tavram paused. He had told Victoria that he would

likely never think of the humans again after leaving her ship. In truth, he had thought of little else.

"Let me tell you, Emperor, of quite a singular empire I encountered."

———

Tessa Baum glanced in the corner of the compartment. The security team had to restrain Best Wishes, seized by another of his fits. One of them persisted in attempting to help him eat, but to little purpose. The Dirregaunt commander was no longer lucid. From what she could gather from the crew he had willingly taken in the light of the ion cloud, driven himself mad in his pursuit of perfect clarity. At times he was almost alert, but after the *Condor* had escaped he had suffered a total breakdown, much like the ship. She grimaced. His matron should have named him Pitiful Creature. In truth she wasn't much better off. Her fever had broken, but now shivering fits wracked her weakened body. Her hip throbbed constantly, too tender to touch and lancing agony whenever her vacuum suit brushed against it.

She was with Dutiful Heiress, now the ranking officer and acting commander of what was left of the *Springdawn*. The fore quarter or so of the ship bereft of engines, food, shuttles, and only dwindling life support from the remaining plant matter had nevertheless evaded the Malagath sensors several days prior. A useless navigation center provided a cramped shelter to the thirty lethargic survivors in this area of the ship, a pale shadow of the *Springdawn's* former compliment of crew. Other pockets of survivors might exist elsewhere, but no one was willing to find out. Huddled together for warmth they waited for death of one kind or another.

She could come and go as she pleased; The Dirregaunt

were barely cognizant of their own surroundings, let alone her. But to where? Half the remaining hulk was in vacuum. She'd searched it and brought what supplies she could find, though most of the Dirregaunt refused to touch them. Her protein reservoirs were empty going on four days now, and her waste recyclers past toxicity levels that would give her sepsis if she didn't starve to death first or die from the after effects of the infection. She had sores anywhere the vacuum suit chafed against her skin. Even these top-of-the-line suits were never meant to be worn more than a few days at the extreme. She felt disgusting, and remarked not for the first time at the futility of worrying how she smelled and how greasy her hair must be while marooned on a derelict dreadnought surrounded by xenos.

Dutiful Heiress was barking commands at the broken crew, and was being largely ignored. What point was there in holding command of a dead ship? She clung to the vestiges of power granted by her birth in the ruling caste. It was a pointless endeavor.

Tessa settled back against the bulkhead. She was weak, starving even. She wondered if she would die before the new commander would stop squawking. She closed her eyes and tried to ignore the knotting in her stomach and the throb at her hip.

She dozed, unsure for how long, before she realized the chatter in her helmet wasn't a computerized translation of Dirregaunt speech.

A radio transmission.

The line crackled with an intermittent voice, "eceived . . . ELT beacon . . . ay location."

She grabbed at the emergency locator on her harness, she had activated it days ago on a whim, knowing Captain Marin had no way of coming back for her.

"Here," she mumbled through gummy, dry lips, "Here I'm here, Tessa Baum of the *Condor*. Location incoming."

She stood carefully and turned to Dutiful Heiress, grabbing her by the arm. "Is the communication suite still functional?" She demanded.

Startled, the Dirregaunt's ears twitched, their version of a nod. "Good," said Tessa, "Send out a distress call with our current location."

"Why?" asked Dutiful Heiress, clearly confused.

"You want to get off this wreck or not?" asked Tessa. The Dirregaunt officer looked skeptical, or at least Tessa assumed it was a skeptical look, but she handled the task herself. There was a shudder as the omnidirectional signal propagated through the hull with its superluminal message. The static in her ear dulled for a few moments, then cleared completely.

"Marine, this is Captain Jackson of the *Huxley*. Have fix on your position. Looks like you could use a lift, trooper."

Tessa grinned, "I hope you've got space in your holds, Captain. This wreck is ten kinds of hot," she said. She looked over at the former commander of the *Springdawn*, now practically comatose and staring at the bulkhead. "I hope you have some brig space, too. I got someone here you're gonna want."

———

"The new chief engineer is aboard, Skipper," said Huian Wong.

Victoria stepped through the airlock into the cargo bay of the *Condor*. The ship had been beat to hell when she'd got it the first time, and she hadn't improved the state of things much. Her bird would always carry the scars of humanity's progress.

"So you decided to stick around. Who'd we get?"

Huian consulted her tablet. Christ she looked just like her mother when she did that. "Davis Prescott, chief engineer of the *U.E.N. Washington*."

"Prescott, eh? Well he's no Yuri, but the *Washington's* got a good rep for a Yank ship. I've heard he wrenches pretty good."

"Is that all you've heard?"

"Watch it, Huian," said Victoria as they climbed up to the middle decks. Workmen were carrying outdated sensor components past as they squeezed into the conn. Carillo saluted her from the XO's chair as he fiddled with the new interfaces. As if he'd ever use them underway.

"Sorry, Captain. I didn't mean to suggest . . ."

Victoria laughed, sliding onto her captain's couch. She looked around at the familiar screens, repeaters, piping, and cables. This was her home, her house, and her life.

"Huian, you may be a wretched little S&C spy, but you handled the *Condor* and kept your cool while we stared down Big Three and lived." She paused.

"You're a Vulture now, call me Vick."

ACKNOWLEDGEMENTS

When I started writing Vick's Vultures it was at a low point in my life, surrounded by eddies of loss and opportunity. I spent those summer days in a cramped, hot room. Every morning I was awoken by the sounds of construction, and every night I sweat as my computer competed with the west-facing window for who could keep me warmer. I had just finished the first draft of Devilbone and was ready to cut my teeth on the world of Science Fiction.

At the time, I knew I would be a self-published author. I would do all my own editing, my own covers, and my own marketing. I am happy, in this, to be proven wrong. When I began writing, it was in secret, and I told no one who did not know me by a pen name that I had written a single word until I had finished my first novel. It had no dedication page and no one to acknowledge because, apart from a critique group, it was written in near vacuum.

Now, I have the support of a small network of authors and the advantage of a small but passionate publisher standing beside me. My writing is exposed for all to see, and has found a warm reception. Those who helped it along the way deserve my gratitude.

First and foremost, I'd like to thank Eric and Colin of Parvus Press for believing in my work and for taking such a huge chance on making Vick's Vultures the "tip of the PP spear". Perhaps I should consider rephrasing that.

I'd also like to thank my editor, John Adamus, who upon telling me that my novel was in good shape handed me back a manuscript with over 300 revisions and corrections. Together we hammered Vick's Vultures into a lean, fighting book.

Possibly the hardest aspect of control to surrender was that of the cover. Having come from an illustration background it was very hard for me to sign off on another artist representing my work. But Tom Edwards has captured the feel and tone of 60,000 words in a single image in such a way that I know I could not have matched. And so (not as reluctantly as I would have expected) I say thank you.

Lastly, I'd like to thank those close to me who encouraged my work, whether having read it or sight unseen, and who never doubted my ability to tackle such an undertaking. Especially my sister, Katie, whom I waited far too long to include in my writing process.

Scott Warren
July 6, 2016

ABOUT THE AUTHOR

Scott Warren got his start in writing while living in Washington during the summer of 2014 when he entered the world of speculative fiction by writing Sorcerous Crimes Division, followed shortly by Vick's Vultures.

Scott blends aspects of classic military fantasy and science fiction with a modern, streamlined writing style to twist tired tropes into fresh ideas. He believes in injecting a healthy dose of adventure into the true-to-life grit and grime that marks the past decade of science fiction, while still embracing the ideas that made science fiction appeal to so many readers.

As a UAV Pilot and former submariner, Scott draws on his military and aviation experiences to bring authenticity to his writing while keeping it accessible to all readers. Scott is also an artist, contributing his skills to board games, role playing games, and his own personal aerial photography galleries.

Scott currently lives in Huntsville, Alabama. Visit Scott on the web: http://scottwarrenscd.blogspot.com/ and follow him on Twitter: @ScottWarrenSCD

COMING SOON FROM PARVUS PRESS

Court of Twilight
by Mareth Griffith

Six months ago, Ivy stumbled into the deal of a lifetime - great rent in a posh Dublin neighborhood and a flatmate, Demi, who was only a little weird. It didn't matter that the flat was packed with exotic plants or that she couldn't touch Demi's cookware.

Now Demi's missing though, there are strange men hiding in the flower boxes, and Demi may have drawn the attention of an ancient evil intent on striking her down. Flatmates, what can you do?

Ivy dives into a myterious hidden Dublin, discovering that the longer she stays in, the more she risks losing the world she always knew. How can she save Demi without losing herself?

Court of Twilight is a suspenseful, twisting contemporary fantasy from a talented new author that explores and tests the bonds of friendship and family while taking the reader on a journey across time and between worlds.

Winter 2017

DO YOU LIKE FREE BOOKS?

www.ParvusPress.com

Sign up for the Parvus Press mailing list to win advance reader copies of upcoming titles, enter contests for free books, and follow our growing family of authors. We hate cluttered inboxes as much as you do and we'll only reach out when we've got something worth your while to share.

Thanks for being Parvus People!

THIS PAGE UNINTENTIONALLY LEFT BLANK

CPSIA information can be obtained
at www.ICGtesting.com
Printed in the USA
LVOW12s2302260916

506317LV00001B/30/P